Jill Paton Walsh was educated at St Michael's Convent, North Finchley, and at St Anne's College, Oxford. Her adult novels are *Lapsing* (1986), *A School For Lovers* (1989), *Knowledge of Angels* (1994), which was shortlisted for the 1994 Booker Prize, and *Goldengrove Unleaving* (1997). She has also won many awards for her children's literature, including the Whitbread Prize, the Universe Prize and the Smarties Award.

She has three children and lives in Cambridge.

Praise for *Knowledge of Angels*:

'An allegory for today and yesterday . . . A beautiful and unsettling moral fiction about virtue and intolerance'
Observer

'An irresistible blend of intellect and passion . . . novels of ideas come no better than this sensual example'
Mail on Sunday

'A compelling mediaeval fable, written from the heart and melded to a driving narrative which never once loses its tremendous pace'
Guardian

'An enchanting, beautifully crafted tale . . . a compelling mediaeval fable about universal conflicts'
West Australian

'A truly unforgettable book. Paton Walsh writes as though she has knowledge of angels herself'
Herald S

Also by Jill Paton Walsh

KNOWLEDGE OF ANGELS
LAPSING
A SCHOOL FOR LOVERS
GOLDENGROVE UNLEAVING

and published by Black Swan

THE
SERPENTINE CAVE

Jill Paton Walsh

BLACK SWAN

THE SERPENTINE CAVE
A BLACK SWAN BOOK : 0 552 99720 X

Originally published in Great Britain by Doubleday,
a division of Transworld Publishers Ltd

PRINTING HISTORY
Doubleday edition published 1997
Black Swan edition published 1998

Black Swan Books are published by Transworld Publishers Ltd,
61–63 Uxbridge Road, London W5 5SA,
in Australia by Transworld Publishers (Australia) Pty Ltd,
15–25 Helles Avenue, Moorebank, NSW 2170
and in New Zealand by Transworld Publishers (NZ) Ltd,
3 William Pickering Drive, Albany, Auckland.

Reproduced, printed and bound in Great Britain by
Cox & Wyman Ltd, Reading, Berks.

To Margaret Freeman with admiration

THE SERPENTINE CAVE

There were three women in the room. One lying on the bed under a white sheet, eyes closed. One wearing a white coat, studying a bleeping monitor, among an assembly of strange devices on an aluminium trolley. The third staring fixedly out of the window.

A bare window; if there were curtains nobody had troubled to draw them across the naked night. A characterless window; no dividers, just glass, and so high up nobody could have looked in on the neon-lit drama within the room. Marian had been looking out for some time, ever since a faintly sulphurous ribbon across the glazed screen of darkness had caught her drifting, disorientated attention. This was dawn. Very slowly the streak of dirty pallor across the view brightened, and took on a yellow hue. It was finely laced with the black branches of still leafless trees. A simplifying mist had left them outlined. Behind the visible trees were more, softly obliterated, and a slight swelling of the rolling arable land that in Cambridgeshire passed for a hill. The hospital lawns below the window were white with spring frost, and gently steaming with drifting strands of mist.

The bleeping monitor counted down the onset of a threatening day. Marian wished it could stop. It did not.

She turned to the doctor, and began to speak, but the doctor at once laid a finger on her lips, and shook her head. She beckoned, and they withdrew together into the corridor.

'What has happened?' asked Marian, though on one level she wanted to tell, rather than ask. She had opened the front door, calling, unsurprised to find no answer and nothing ready. To find the sink full of unwashed dishes, and the usual reek of turpentine competing with the slightly meaty smell of the dishwasher, partly loaded. She had called again, and climbed the steps into the barn that her mother used as a studio, and there had found the slumped body, alive and making awful noises – a monologue of groans and garbled ramblings.

'Your mother has had a stroke,' said the doctor. 'A serious one, this time.'

'This time? I didn't know—'

'Then we can assume that earlier ones, if any, were slight. Perhaps your mother concealed it from you. People sometimes do.'

'Yes – well – but now?'

'I can't tell you very much. She may recover; people do quite often recover almost fully from a stroke. They may regain movement in the paralysed side; with therapy they can often recover some speech. But to be frank with you, at your mother's age . . . there will be some recovery, if she lives long enough. How much, we must wait and see. I am so sorry.'

'If she lives long enough?'

'At her age, you see, Mrs Easton, and after such a severe stroke, she may well have another, within a few days or weeks.'

'I see. Can we do anything?'

'We can make her comfortable. We can keep her here

for a while, and then if no further incident occurs, and her condition stabilizes, we would eventually discharge her and you can look for therapists. Perhaps a nursing home . . . One thing I should warn you about, if I may – your mother has not lost her power to hear and understand you, just because she has lost the power of speech.'

'Warn me?'

'That she can understand you. People sometimes say the most tactless things, even cruel things, because they haven't fully realized that the patient may be upset, perhaps more easily than before, when they can't respond.'

Marian nodded, and returned to the room.

It had been transformed in her absence, in two ways. The horizontal sun had torn through its wrappings of mist, and was lighting the room with a luridly golden light. It had eclipsed the neon strip lights on the ceiling, over-whelming their chilly accuracy with a rival vision, in which Marian's mother lay under a sheet of pale primrose, her face jaundiced, the monitor screen had faded to an indecipherable dimness, and every metal surface in the room – the bedstead, the trolley, the machinery – was dramatically gilded. The window now offered a prospect of egg-shell blue sky, scattered all over with pink-gold puffy small clouds like a baroque ceiling.

But the other transformation was more striking. The patient's eyes were open, in an unfocussed vertical stare.

'Talk to her,' the doctor said.

Marian was seized with a hideous embarrassment, almost revulsion, flinching at the thought of talking *at* her mother, the-no-reply-possible situation transforming conversation into an exhibitionist monologue, or a horrible manipulation, like that of the 'carer' saying, 'Come along, Granny, time for your bath, don't be naughty, now!' Or worse. Marian had heard worse. To say anything at all to someone who cannot offer any reply seemed like a form of contempt.

But the doctor was standing there, waiting.

'Mother?' said Marian. 'I'll clean your brushes when I get back . . .'

And in the silence that followed she had time to feel foolish. She had been subliminally expecting a reply. And – how horribly revealing! She had made a placatory offering. Her mother found her useless in most ways, but had said once or twice that she was good at cleaning brushes. Was this what it would be? When the other cannot reply one simply haemorrhages self-revelation into the silence? She tried again. 'It's thick frost. Bad for the plants, I'm afraid.' For the early spring had tempted the plants to put out tender tipping buds. Now the blooms would unfold with frost burn . . . Nothing to be done about that, of course. 'But it does look pretty, don't you think?'

The woman in the bed uttered a polysyllabic grunt, and very slightly turned her head towards the window.

'Good!' said the doctor. 'She has a little movement in the neck, already. Good. And she answered you – you realize – she did answer, it's just that we can't decipher what the answer meant.'

'So what else is new?' said Marian, bitterly.

'Pardon?' said the doctor. 'Look, I'm leaving her with you now. Just keep talking to her.'

But the urge to silence was overmastering. Marian's moment of revulsion had given way to a rueful amusement. Nothing was much changed, then; she would be burdened with the need to talk, to keep up relations, to bid in one way after another for her mother's attention; her mother would reply if at all in grunts or monosyllables, her attention always directed elsewhere. At least, now, she could not simply walk away! Marian remembered numerous times in the past . . . half-way through the big party she had organized for her mother's eightieth birthday, mother had disappeared, and been found eventually, sitting in the hotel car-park, balancing herself on a bollard in a biting wind, sketching the half-frozen lake in the grounds. And long before that, in the middle of Marian's wedding reception, the bride's mother could not be found when the speeches were being made – she had retreated to her studio and resumed painting. And even longer ago, she had left the guests at Marian's seventh birthday party unsupervised while she worked, and had taken quite calmly the awful results of the jelly-throwing riot which had ensued. But tiny Marian had felt abandoned to the barbarians . . .

'Well, Mother, I can say what I want to you, now,' she said softly. She had to say something, since she was enjoined to speak.

And that remark, floating unanswered in the silence, punctuated by the bleeping monitor, brought to Marian's mind the other sense in which she could say anything she liked to her mother, and always had been able to. Indeed Marian's entire class at school had obtained their un-usually accurate and extensive knowledge of sex, male dispositions and physiology, consequences and contra-ception by getting Marian to ask the taboo questions of her mother, and relay the frank replies. It had not occurred to Marian till many years later that these questions might have misrepresented her to her mother, had she assumed a personal need-to-know basis for them. They had been both knowing questions, and, in Marian's mouth inno-cent, technical, as unloaded of emotion as questions about the internal combustion engine would have been.

The room was suffocatingly hot for someone wearing winter clothes. No doubt for the patient under the starched sheet it was just right . . . and Marian had not slept that night, and was soon drowsing in the stiff little pseudo-leather chair in the corner of the room.

Later Marian's grown children arrived. Toby and Alice had driven themselves up from London, starting early. Marian had not expected them – she would not have expected them to be able to extricate themselves from complex lives for any emergency of her own. Alice came straight to Marian, leaned over the chair, twined her slender arms round Marian's shoulders, laid a cool cheek against her mother's and said softly, 'Hi, there, Mum. Love you.'

Toby went to the bedside, and took up his grand-mother's slack hand in his own. A sudden convulsion seized and twisted Stella's face – her mouth moved lop-sidedly, one side drooping, Marian thought at first, in pain. Then she realized that this rictus was now her mother's smile – her mother was smiling at Toby, and Toby was weeping, his tears falling on their linked hands.

Alice moved across to the bed, and took her grand-mother's other hand. Marian watched her children, amazed as always by their beauty and grace. She could see them normally for normal purposes, but secretly also always saw them this way – her children, aureoled by love. And if they made her feel bypassed, short-circuited, if the directness of their love for Stella shamed her, she deserved it. For she had not herself thought to offer tears, or touching, only a few stiff sentences.

Toby wiped his cheeks dry abruptly with the backs of his hands, and said, 'Don't worry, Gran, we'll look after Mother for you!'

The very last thing that had occurred to Marian in this situation was that anyone needed to look after *her*.

Toby was right, though. When the nurses gently shepherded them out of the room, saying that the patient needed quiet, telling Marian that she needed sleep, suggesting that they came back in the evening, she was lost. She managed to walk as far as the reception area, with its shops and lights, and throngs of people, and the bevies of synthetically smiling clerks and helpers – then she couldn't quite think what she was doing, or where they were going.

'What time is it?' she asked.

'It's not as late as it feels, Mum. Only eleven-thirty. Where are we going?'

'Back to Gran's – Gran's spare rooms, unless you'd rather we looked for a hotel?' Toby said.

'Which would you rather?' said Alice, gently.

'Gran's will be best; there are things we must do . . . people to tell,' she said.

'Not before you've slept.'

'But . . .' She began to protest. But she felt so dazed, so weak, that suddenly she gave in. She let them lead her, and they took charge. Toby drove; she sat in the back seat of his car, and fell so deeply asleep that she didn't wake when they arrived and he switched off the ignition. By the time they woke her they had put sheets on the spare-room bed, and turned back the corner of the blankets, and there was a cup of tea on the bedside table. They had even, she discovered, as having stripped to her underwear she gratefully slid into the bed, put a hot-water bottle between the sheets. As she had so often in the past done for them – the unfamiliar inversion of familiar kindness struck her briefly as astonishing, like watching the shift and tilt of some great balance-beam – and then she slept.

Downstairs her children sat at the kitchen table, talking together, their voices softened partly so as not to wake Marian, partly from the sense of doom that surrounded them.

'Mum won't want to go home while Gran's like that,' said Alice. 'It's such a long way away. She'll want to hang around and visit.'

'I expect she'll manage all right if she has to,' said Toby. 'But it would be hard on her. I was thinking I might stay over for a day or two.'

'How can you? Won't your precious firm lose millions the moment you take your eyes off the dealing screens?'

'Listen to you! And no doubt you're about to drop everything and everybody and tear off to some rehearsal. For some stupid concert with wads of unsold tickets that loses more money every time than I can make in an hour—'

'Toby, we musn't do this. We mustn't quarrel now.'

They looked at each other across the kitchen table.

'Find a time and place for it later, you mean?'

'Probably. But for the moment in spite of your unkind assumptions, I am staying around.'

'Nothing to rehearse for?'

'Don't *probe*, Toby. Just accept.'

'OK. The place is a bit insanitary, isn't it? Should we clear up?'

'Someone will have to, some time.'

'Social services would take one look at this, and decide Gran would have to be put in a home. It's yucky!'

'It always was. And we never used to mind,' she said. 'But just the same . . . and I bet there's nothing to eat.'

Investigation revealed one quite good-looking lamb chop in the refrigerator, several packets of powdered soup, some mildewed bread, and a large jar of porridge oats. They began to laugh.

'Hush!' said Toby, shutting the kitchen door.

'Oh, Gran!' said Alice. 'Gran as ever!'

'I expect one can live for months on porridge,' said Toby.

'Porridge and a lamb chop – don't forget the lamb chop!' Their laughter was fed on recollections of desperate meals eaten in Stella's house in long ago holidays – wild forays to the fish-and-chip shop, mounds of baked beans topped with one rasher of bacon between the three of them, once – once only – potatoes stolen from the field beside the house; these gruesome menus varied on rare occasions when Stella had sold a painting, by sudden excursions to posh restaurants in Cambridge.

'Well, be fair – she wasn't expecting company – she didn't expect to be dying . . .' said Toby. Laughter stopped at once.

'I'd better start by going shopping,' said Alice.

'OK,' said Toby. 'I'll ring Dad – hadn't I better? I mean he ought to know about it, even if . . . And then I'll tackle that.' He pulled a face at the mound of dishes in the sink.

'Dad will think himself well out of this,' said Alice. 'I'll be as quick as poss.'

'Fine. Do you need money?'

'Toby, even viola players can afford food.'
As the door closed behind her, he went for the phone.

Marian woke as a small child. For a long moment she lay
warmly awake, slightly puzzled as to her exact whereabouts, as she had so often been before. But it was
indubitably childhood. The battered and faded familiarity
of the chest-of-drawers, the bedside alarm clock, leaning
backwards on angled legs, and topped with a miniature
structure like a bicycle bell – the worn coverlet stretching
over her – all these things which had been hers before she
left home carried her backwards and displaced her sense of
self. Even more vivid was the rapturously sweet sense of
other people in the house – footfalls, quiet voices, a door
closing, a few notes played on the piano – that wonderful
sensation of a house which contained others, in which
other lives also were sheltered and flowing, in which one's
own silence was not silence, one's own stillness was not
stillness – how she had missed it all this time living alone!
There was the violently reminiscent faint penetrating
odour of turps . . . only when Marian moved did she feel,
astonished, the adult weight and length of her grown
limbs, and come to herself again.

Of course, she was herself the grown-up; the children
were downstairs, and the children themselves were grown
up. She got up and went down to the kitchen. There she
found Alice stirring a pot on the stove, and Toby rinsing
brushes and laying them out on kitchen paper to dry.

The room was transformed; the dishwasher was
rumbling away on an umpteenth load, and the dresser

was bright with clean dishes. The floor had been washed, the counters wiped, a vase with dead flowers now displayed some prospective daffodils with tightly rolled yellow-tipped buds. She perceived with astonishment their competence, their willingness, Toby especially, doing the brushes.

'I was going to do that, Toby,' she said.

'Done,' he said, grinning. 'Gran always said I was good at it.'

'Did she? I thought I was the only one she let do it.'

'More fool you two,' said Alice tartly. 'I made sure I did it very badly, myself. I hope you like garlic, Mum.'

'Have you done supper, darling?'

'I thought we had better eat before visiting this evening – don't you?'

Marian realized she was ravenously hungry, and eagerly agreed. And yet her appetite was a chimera which faded after a mouthful, leaving her feeling vacant and sick.

'There, Ma,' said Toby, 'it doesn't matter.'

'Alice cooked it . . .' said Marian sadly, looking at the buttery, garlicky spaghetti on her plate.

'It's only spaghetti, Mum,' said Alice, untroubled. 'Shall I make you soup instead?'

Her children's kindness was too much for her. She sat tongue-tied, overcome.

'Oh, there, Ma, don't take on,' said Toby, and then, absurdly, 'What's the matter?'

'It's too late!' she said; the words had risen to her lips before reaching her conscious mind.

'Too late for what?' asked Alice.

'Too late to ask her things – all the things I was going to ask her, and she was always busy, so busy, and I didn't ask and now she can't tell me . . . Oh, I left it too late!'

Her son and her daughter both put down their forks and looked at her tenderly.

'What did you want to ask, Ma?' said Toby softly. His eyes met Alice's, wide and full of unspoken warning. They were both expecting an answer; they both knew what they thought she would have wanted to know; she must have wanted to know about her father, their missing grandfather, never named, never spoken of, whose absence had left their mother lacking some sort of sixth sense, whose absence had led in the fullness of time – or so they saw it – to the defection of their own father.

But what Marian said, at last, was nothing about her father. It was: 'Oh, where were the beaches? Where was the Serpentine Cave?'

Someone had been there wearing a dress printed with bright blotchy flowers. Pansies, printed pansies. The dress had smelled of laundry – that washing line, open-air smell. Marian's face had been leaning against the dress, as she was carried down. It must – surely? – have been Stella's arms she was carried in; but if she rigorously divided memory from supposition, she would have to admit to remembering only the dress, not the wearer. They had to climb down a steep cliff-face. The cliff-top grass was shining and slippery. Marian was passed to another person, who held her firmly, and carried her down to the roaring shore.

But on the beach she had been alone. There were huge cliffs, and enormous pillars of rock, standing up out of the sea. It was a rowdy sea, with great glassy walls of waves rolling towards her, and falling into flat, speeding, lacy shallows at the last minute. She had been afraid of the sea; it was too big for her, here. She had backed away up the beach, towards the mouth of a cave. The cave glistened and shone. Down at her eye-level it had polished walls, smooth and coloured. Dark green and dark red, and speckled grey-white, marbled together like the lump of used Plasticine rolled into a ball when she finished modelling, but shiny where the Plasticine was dull. She had touched the gleaming rock, and walked further into the cave.

It was like a cave in dreams; or, perhaps, it was the cave that afterwards she dreamed of. The roof was rough and dark, and the floor was of smoothest golden sand, cool, firm and gritty under her bare feet. The polished planes of the walls were like coloured tombstones. And across the door of the cave there beat with slow violence a slowly rising tide. Right at the back of the cave facing her was a surface of particular beauty, deep red, with snaking lines of white and green. It was not darker back there, so she walked further in. And soon she saw that the cave was L-shaped; the light at the back was falling from another entrance, which gave out onto a prospect of more bright sunlit sand. So she went out by this other way.

Beyond the cave she was walking on a golden causeway towards another mass of offshore rock, taller than houses, and topped with grassy green. And in this mysterious place the sea was on both sides, on her right and on her left hand; roaring towards her in huge toppling glassy towers. She had thought the sea was always on one side, and the land the other. There were gulls calling overhead, and some of them began to call her name, screaming from some distance off. She went back into the cave, from which her own footprints led out to where she stood. But when she had walked back through it she found her way blocked, and she doubled back again through the cave.

The spine of sand beyond it was narrow now; it was awash with joining waters, running up the slopes and clapping themselves together in the middle. She ran for a little dry patch, and at once found no way back. She stood islanded, and said to the ocean, 'Don't!'

Someone came. A man came wading knee deep, shouting, and lifted and carried her. The only way possible, which was out to the cliff island ahead of them. He scrambled up higher and higher, pushing and dragging her with him, until they were on a flat grassy ledge, quite a wide one, with pinks and lady's slipper growing in the grass. He crouched down with her in the wind shelter of a rock.

There must have been a sunset, but she did not remember it. All these memories had been sorted out long ago into some sort of sequence – a sequence full of darkness and puzzlement, but more orderly than the broken, intensely vivid visual 'stills' from which it had been assembled. It had been dark and cold. She remembered a great moon sailing up out of the sea, and icing the scene with faint but lucid light.

When she said, 'I'm hungry,' the man said, 'I'm sorry.' When she asked for her mother he pointed at a tiny point of bright flickering orange light, a fire burning on the facing shore, and said that was where Stella was. When she said she was cold, he took her on his knee, opened his jacket, and buttoned her into it, and she could feel his heartbeat. Now and then he unbuttoned his jacket, made her stand up, made her walk about, run, even. She didn't want to. There were bright stars. Below them the moonlit water was softly clamouring.

How long was it? – she could not tell – before the waves rolled back, and reluctantly exposed a ribbon of wet, dimly visible sand? It changed its mind between one wavebreak and the next, uncovering and recovering the precarious link to the land. The man helped her down, and held her hand as they ran across between wave and wave, getting wet; but she remembered it not seeming cold – she was bone frozen already.

There were people round the fire on the cliff. They had blankets, and hot soup. They wore coats and scarves. They would not let Marian and the man come near the fire. And Stella was angry with her.

When she recovered enough to explain herself, Toby and Alice received what fragments of this memory she told over for them with considerable interest.

'They kept you away from the fire because it's dangerous to warm up too quickly,' said Alice. 'I learned that in First Aid.'

'Is it?' said Marian. 'Yes, you're right; I think I knew that – but I never connected it, somehow.' She was bemused; she could actually feel the faint ghost of resentment, which clung about the memory like the fusty air in an old chest, dispersing at Alice's breezy interpretation.

'Was the man our grandfather, do you think?' asked Toby. Somehow he avoided saying 'your father' which seemed too nakedly tactless.

'I don't know,' said Marian. 'Don't you think I would know, if he had been?'

'Perhaps if it was wartime he had been away for ages and he was home on leave,' suggested Alice.

But Marian thought that somehow even if he had been

strange to her, surely Stella would have told her that this was her father – surely such a thing as that could not have been unspoken. Though of course, with Stella one could not know. She might or might not have dealt with her child as another woman would.

It had always been a problem. What seemed natural to Stella, needing no explanation or excuse, seemed, often, weird and arbitrary to those around her, including her daughter. Nothing much, on the other hand, seemed weird to Stella, except her daughter. And on that recipro-cal strangeness Marian had time to reflect in the days that followed, as she came faithfully to sit by her mother's bedside, and think of things that might be said into silence:

'Toby cleaned your brushes . . . Your neighbours have been asking after you . . . the vicar called; I told him you were here, I hope you didn't mind? Did he come? . . .' And when nothing brought a grunt, a flicker of reaction, a turn of the head, greatly daring she asked, 'Mother, where was the Serpentine Cave?'

And then there was time to wonder, sitting in the room heavy with silence, on the little hard armchair facing the bed, on where it could have been, out of dozens of places possible, and why Marian did not now know where it was.

Stella had moved. She would move in somewhere – a little house in Concarneau, a flat in Rome, a concrete villa in the Algarve, a house in Argenteuil, a farmhouse near Avignon, an apartment in Siena – Marian lost count. Stella would enrol Marian in the local school, and leave her struggling with strange teachers, wary children, a gobbledygook language. She, Stella, would plunge furiously into the local scenery and paint it. Some time later, often when Marian had found a friend of some sort, knew the way to the local shops, had mastered the unfamiliar coins, Stella would suddenly have exhausted the landscape, and would move on. Stella did sometimes sell pictures; she toted them around cafés, she painted portraits which the sitters dutifully bought, she sent some home to England with departing friends who came visiting. But she also abandoned pictures, leaving numbers of them stacked face to the wall in the rooms that they left.

Marian could be reduced to tears, helpless rage in which she screamed and kicked, simply by the sight of a suitcase. And yet there was a consolation. Each new place was so clean and orderly when they moved in. Stella rented places that smelled of furniture wax, or of the coastal air. The walls were often white, the bedlinen worn fine with age and use. Even Stella could not create chaos – unwashed dishes lying on the trestle among the paints, the smell of turpentine, the clothes cast everywhere and hanging out of half open drawers like the aftermath of a burglary, the twisted and deformed tubes of paint, with caps forgotten, or dried-on solid, the stale loaves mustily green in the bins – absolutely instantly. Even Stella took a week or so to reduce her surroundings to the familiar condition of home. That week partly reconciled her daughter to the arduous business of learning local words, coinage, faces all over again.

For Marian had yearned for order. For things kept clean and put away after use. For spaces which specialized, so that cooking was confined to the kitchen, sleeping to the bedrooms; so that the toothbrushes could reliably be found in the bathroom, and coats and shopping baskets in the hall, hanging up. So that there should be a room, called the sitting room, *la salle de séjour*, the drawing room, *il salotto*, the lounge even, dedicated to the comfortable doing of nothing whatever, so that it could be calm, with clean cushions, folded newspapers, books in a bookcase – a room in which it appeared possible that people sometimes just sat. Above all, Marian longed for painting to be kept in a studio. For there not to be wet surfaces everywhere, for there to be a possibility at least of having no paint at all on her clothes, especially the ones she wore to school.

None of these things mattered to Stella. She thought about her paintings, and the light.

Once, after a particularly painful quarrel – for these differences between mother and daughter did not go unenunciated – Stella tried to explain herself, excuse herself to her daughter. Marian could not now remember what the triggering quarrel was about; not surprisingly her childhood was a blur to her now. She could barely remember which place was which . . . *Mother, where was the Serpentine Cave?* Perhaps they had quarrelled about a move. No – it must have been the occasion when she had been brought home in disgrace, having run amuck in a French classroom, bloodied the nose of a fellow pupil, refused to sit down . . .

The teacher had asked her what her father did for a living.

'I have no father.'

'Your mother, then?'

Groping for the word, Marian said, '*Elle est une artiste.*'

The other children tittered. But it was because the teacher had laughed too that Marian went berserk, and lashed out at the boy sitting beside her.

'But what should I have said?' Marian had asked her mother, as later they mulled over the calamity together, sitting facing each other across a table covered in congealed paint and abandoned coffee cups.

Stella had fetched her *Harrap's French Dictionary*, and consulted it. '*Une femme peintre,*' she said. 'It seems I am *une femme peintre*. But it's somewhat obscure. I might be *une artiste peintre*. But perhaps that sounds too like the artiste as in trapeze artiste, singer, stripper, performing seal, performing whore, or whatever it is you accidentally called me . . .'

And Marian had wailed at Stella, 'Why can't you be like other people's mothers?'

Stella had not answered at first. She had wiped her hands on her overall, leaving a smear of flake-white on the blue canvas, moved across the room to the little bench that served as a kitchen, lifted the kettle off the gas ring, tipped the dregs of something out of a chipped mug, made herself a Camp Coffee, brought it to the table, and sat down facing her sullen and accusing child.

'You see, Mara,' she said, using Marian's self-given, lisping baby name, 'there isn't any point in living just to live. In making oneself rich and comfortable and then just *being* rich and comfortable. What would it be *for*? Things have to be for something.'

At the time Marian couldn't see anything she herself was for. Her answers, when they came, would be Toby and Alice, and Stella would have applied the same brutal query to them.

'You find something to live for,' said Stella, 'and it takes priority. It must. Painting, for me. Only that.'

'What about me?' Marian had asked.

'You'll find something,' her mother had said. 'There are lots of things.' But Marian had been asking a more dangerous question.

'And are they all arty, these things?' she had retorted, bitterly. '*I* think to make your life worthwhile something useful would be better!'

'Then you will do something useful. But useful things, you know, are only for use.'

'What's for supper?' young Marian had asked, baffled, and playing her ace card. Even her mother had to eat.

At bedtime that day Stella had arrived to kiss Marian goodnight – she did not usually bother – and said, 'I suppose you don't fancy that school any more. I think I might go and paint Italy for a while.'

'Mother,' Marian had said, 'isn't there anything to paint in England?'

Later shame was replaced by pride. An art teacher in the secondary school, in a mundane inland suburb of Brighton where they had fetched up, gave Marian a life of Van Gogh. The story transformed Stella's total inability to sell paintings in England from a badge of failure into a possible waymark on the path to glory. Marian's classmates at this stage of life mostly despised their mothers, whose neat homes, dated taste in clothes, and preference for dreadful dance music put them beyond every possible pale. The chaos and freedom of Marian's life impressed them. And she was in the grip of a fierce and partisan admiration for her mother. Stella was a heroine, a self-sacrificing, aspiring martyr to her art. The desperate hand-to-mouth economy of mother and daughter, the near hardship they endured as the unsold paintings accumulated on top of wardrobes and under beds, the all too obvious disinterested lack of material greed which characterized Stella's life-choices further impressed her daughter. Marian's admiration was compounded by the knowledge that she herself would never be so noble; there was no cause or skill of anything like comparable difficulty and elevation that she, Marian, wished to serve or acquire. She was going to be ordinary.

The admiration while it lasted choked up her words, and further complicated her life with her mother. Had Stella noticed it? Marian doubted that she had.

There was a day she remembered, a bright summer day of the glassy light in which Brighton specialized, when Stella had driven the car up Ditchling Beacon, with a picnic in a basket along with all her gear. Marian had brought a book. She had spread out the rug, and lain on her stomach, chin propped in hands, book open on the grass in front of her, looking out over the view. The South Downs had seemed like a solid sea, made of green swelling waves, advancing like a great tide and stopped by some sudden ancient enchantment. Stella called her, and she lumbered up from the rug. There Stella stood, with two easels set up, two plain sized boards propped ready. Stella was wearing a white floppy hat, and a pale brown overall over her red dress. She held out to her daughter a brush, and a pallet.

'Wouldn't you like, just once, to try?' she had asked.

Marian had looked at the huge prospect, the stilled movement of the crests and troughs of land, the heat haze just faintly now beginning to soften outlines, the light silken movement of wind running on the bowing grass under a sky like translucent bright shadows . . . She remembered the hours of labour, the misery, the striving, the painting over, the abandoned canvases, the subjects tackled again and again which characterized her mother's life. She felt herself to be a tiny, incompetent pigmy, beside *une femme peintre*; and both of them cast away help-lessly on the flood of the beauty of the world.

'No, thanks, Mother,' she said. 'Don't worry, I've brought a book.'

It was later again that shame returned to her. She brought a boy home from college to stay a few days; he wanted to see Brighton. He seemed glamorous and sophisticated to Marian. He had played Hamlet in the college production, and affected an Olivier mode of dress – black polo-necks, and black jeans, and an expression of anguished abstraction. Entering the house, and having penetrated only the front room, he had said, 'God, Marian, whatever are all these daubs? You don't mean to say your mother paid good money for these?'

Marian had not briefed him; had no right to expect him to bite his tongue. His unfeigned contempt opened to her the horrible possibility that in the eyes of the *cognoscenti* her mother was not good – was terrible, even. The young man, on getting further into the house, and perceiving the confusion, the plethora of paintings and the smell of turps, cottoned on, and said not another word about it. He fell over himself to be courteous to Stella, who barely noticed whether he was or not, being as usual deeply engrossed. But taking his leave, three days later, he said to Marian, 'I had no idea. It must be very hard on you.' From then on, of course, it was.

For it is one thing to have been sacrificed in pursuit of the achievements of a genius; quite another to have been neglected and bundled around from place to place, to have had a fragmented education, and endlessly been put second to a duff artist. Marian could forgive her mother her childhood if her mother was brilliant; to have lived through all that for the sake of an obsessional *hobby*, for the sake of badly executed daubs, filled Marian with shame. And rage followed swiftly after.

Rage fuelled escape. Marian went to college, and seldom came home. If this now seemed ungracious to her, sitting watching her mother helpless, and probably dying, she remembered in her own defence how little difference her presence or absence made to Stella. Stella went on working absolutely regardless of who might be in the house, or what they might need for comfort – food, towels, a word of welcome. Late at night she would talk, over a shared whisky, but only about her painting. About Marian's studies she never asked, her palpable incomprehension of her daughter's choice of subject left unspoken.

But then, it occurred to Marian now, perhaps her mother had taken her studies as a silent reproach, as a move in the endless struggle between them. Marian studied pharmaceutical chemistry, a subject requiring neatness, orderly methodology, objectivity and calm. A subject she had thought of as indubitably useful – as far as could be from the hateful uncertainty of art, where a painting could seem valuable beyond all price to one person, and a worthless daub to another person. A drug had a proven and uncontroversial use. Its correct administration helped people. The possibility of iatrogenic illness had not then occurred to her. Only now, her mind drifting across occluded stretches of the past, now misty, now clear, did she remember seeing somewhere a lovely pharmacy window full of gorgeously swelling glass jars, containing a rainbow array of coloured liquids. Had she after all been following an inherited passion for colour and form?

At first Marian and the children were only camped in Stella's house. It was a graceless modern house, much extended, set back from the village green, crouched behind a thick screen of holly hedge, dwarfed by a huge willow tree that spring was turning the colour of tarnished brass. Later it would drift gossamer wispy seeds all over the place like a split eiderdown. Stella had bought the place because it had been built in front of an old barn, a black, clapboard structure which the previous owners had converted into a games room, weather-proofing and insulating the walls, replacing the huge wagon-doors in the sides with enormous windows, and extending the house to meet it, so that there was an indoor way through to it, down a few stairs to the barn level. Here Stella had worked. It was on the stairs into the barn that Marian had found her lying stricken when she came for the weekend.

In the house Toby and Alice settled into the rooms they traditionally had on visits to Stella. Stella's own room was left to Marian. For days they didn't move anything. Apart from the clean kitchen, and the well-stocked fridge, everything was as found; they felt like guests, free to sit, but not to move the chairs. Toby and Alice in turn went down to London, and fetched their books and clothes. But it was a long way home for Marian; she went into Cambridge and bought herself two changes of ordinary clothes to make do. They began to take visiting Stella turn and turn about. And after a fortnight they did move chairs into the sitting room – they put an armchair to each side of the fire, and dragged the sofa across the room, so that they could all three sit comfortably.

Comfortably up to a point, that is. Stella's furniture had come from her parents' house, and had been in its day solid and respectable. It had probably come from the best department store in the city in which Stella's father had been a shipping agent, and her mother had become the first lady mayoress. It had seen better days. The sofa had long since collapsed, ruptured by escaping coil springs, and broken webbing, and was covered with piles of cushions to build up the sag. The room satisfied the minimum requirements – there was a fire, there was something to sit on, but everything in it had been used almost to destruction. Also it was spectacularly untidy. There was a bookcase, in which the books were mostly in sets; Victorian novels with the names of Stella's parents on the flyleaves. There was a piano, left open, and with piles of newspapers and art magazines stacked on the dusty keys. An unpleasant smell proved to be a liquefying cauliflower in a plastic supermarket bag full of groceries, put down behind the door and forgotten. The only normal-looking object in the room was a photograph of Toby and Alice taken five years ago, standing on the mantelpiece in a heavily tarnished silver frame. A rather good antique mirror with iridescence creeping across the mercury behind the glass hung over the mantel. No pictures. Oddly, no pictures.

The whole thing had that awful poignancy of a room

not lived in. Apart from the cauliflower, which must have been fairly recent, it had been abandoned for years – it belonged to someone who had no time for sitting rooms. And yet they could not clear it up. Anyone can tidy anyone's kitchen; but tidying all these scattered possessions without obvious rightful places was beyond them. And although it was Stella's absence that the room spoke of; her total indifference to the things most people cared about, her life that went from bed to kitchen to studio, and never came in here; yet to tidy it would have been in some odd sense to obliterate her presence.

Meanwhile, they had to have something to do. Toby rented a television set with a video player, and rented videos from the village shop. They found a local walk along the ridge of a modest rise in the land – the last wrinkle of the chalk crests descending from the uplands to the fen.

'It's a good enough place, I suppose,' said Marian to the children, over supper one night. 'But I can't quite think why it should be here, particularly, that your grandmother settled after so much wandering.'

'To be near someone?' asked Toby.

'Or something,' suggested Alice. 'There were some pictures in Cambridge she liked to look at now and then, I think.'

'There are good pictures in the Fitzwilliam,' offered Toby.

'She had a lot of space here,' said Alice. 'More than she could have afforded in a town.'

The hospital moved Stella into a side room, and then into another wing. She had fallen utterly silent – not a whisper, not a groan came from her sagging mouth. Toby thought he had set up a system. 'She's still *there*,' he said. 'If you ask her to squeeze your hand once for yes, and

34

twice for no, she can answer questions.' But either he was imagining things, or Stella didn't want to answer Marian; and in any case neither *Where were those beaches?* nor *Who was my father?* could be answered yes or no.

On one occasion Marian's visit was interrupted by that of a consultant. He picked up and read the medical notes hanging from the foot of the bed, felt for a pulse, pulled down an eyelid, and said to Marian, 'Do you see any change in her?'

'Only that she is quieter. She seems to have stopped trying to talk.'

'I think she is slipping away from us,' the consultant said. 'Hard to be sure.'

'Is there any hope for her at all?' Marian asked him. 'Any chance at all that she could go home, take up some sort of life again?'

'Realistically, I should say no, I'm afraid. The longer it goes without sign of recovery, the bleaker the prospect.'

'Then how long can this go on?' Marian asked.

'How long can what go on?'

'This terrible state, neither living nor dying.'

'I would tell you if I knew,' he said. 'I suppose – she didn't leave instructions, did she?'

'What sort of instructions?' asked Marian.

'A living will. Her wishes in case just this situation should arise. Or perhaps you can tell us what she would have wanted?'

'I didn't know her well enough for that,' said Marian bleakly.

'People often tell us that,' he said. She was suddenly aware of how gentle his tone was. He was being kind, standing in the corridor on his way to some other calamity, lingering, talking to her. 'You might like to think about it. Talk to other relatives. Go through her papers.'

Marian's expression must have been eloquent.

'It is quite certain she will never look at them again herself,' he said. 'Someone will have to sort things for her.'

'I'll ask the children,' Marian said.

They confabulated sitting round the kitchen table.

'I don't entirely grasp what they want,' said Marian.

'They want permission – written if possible – to stop treating her. Not to resuscitate her if she has a heart attack, not to treat her if she gets pneumonia,' said Toby.

'But surely, they wouldn't . . . ?' Alice said. 'Would they bring her back for that?'

'They'll protect themselves. In case we sue for neglect,' Toby said. 'Believe me.'

'You mean we might have to get her out of there, to let her die?' said Alice, incredulous.

'Did she ever express any opinion about this to either of you?' asked Marian. 'She never did to me.'

Her children looked at her in silence. 'Be merciful, Mum, and forge something,' said Alice.

'Well, let's look first,' said Toby. 'It might be already there.'

'I find,' said Marian slowly, 'it's very difficult. It feels like an intolerable thing to do . . . spying . . . like reading someone's diary by stealth. She would hate it so!'

'You do her an injustice, Ma,' said Toby. 'She was – she is – quite a sensible person.'

'Sensible?' said Marian. 'That's the last word—'

'She didn't want the things most people want,' he said.

'But she was perfectly hard-headed at getting what she did want. I think.'

'Mum, don't worry, though,' said Alice. 'If you don't fancy ransacking the inner sanctums, Toby and I will do it.'

So Marian was sent out into the garden with a book, while her children began, in a sombre mood, to search the house, setting it into some kind of order as they went.

It was that day of the year when suddenly there is a softness in the air, and one needs to be out of doors. Marian pulled a mildewed deck-chair out of the leaking summerhouse, and set it up in deep grass under the apple tree, in the drift of falling petals. The creak of protest it emitted as she sat in it gave way to a deep silence defined by the audibility of bees in the flowering wilderness around her. A gawky overgrown cotoneaster with tiny tight pink blooms was loud with them, over by the sagging fence. A too bright, shifting dapple of leaves and light skittered over the page of her book and made her blink uncomprehendingly at the print. She never had been good at reading out of doors. Besides, she was weighed down with weariness. All the emotion, all the upheaval, the appalling sight of *une femme peintre* laid low like a fallen tree weighed her down, like that other silence at the bedside, defined by the bleeping monitor, or the discreet tap of flat-heeled shoes, approaching, retreating.

And was it fair, to be out here, mooning about, leaving the real task to the children? Grown children, to be sure – but she was aware of needing them, leaning on them, as she could never remember her mother leaning on her. And what were they doing here? How was it they were free to come, and even odder, free to stay? If she did feel it was unfair, she did not feel it enough to get herself out of the deck-chair. She lay still, and closed her eyes. A bird alighting in the leafy mezzanine above her began to sing in melodic bursts of fluent meaningless beauty.

And while reproaching herself for doing nothing, she found she had made decisions. No mother of mine, she had decided, will be shunted off into a nursing home. Of course, she may still be in charge of herself; we may find that living will. But if it is up to me, I shall bring her back here. I will make a bed in the barn, where she can have her working mess around her. I will see her through it – see her out. Whatever a perfect daughter would do, I will do it. She can call in her debts now, and I will make amends. Because of course it is only when I was callow and angry that I thought what lay between us was that she was a bad mother. To her I was a bad daughter. Whatever it was she lived by, I would not see it. What I chose instead she found worthless. It takes two people to make such a discord; if we couldn't do anything else together, we will do her dying together.

This felt more to her like something she had discovered to be true than like a decision in the usual sense, where one feels one might have decided otherwise. It was not negotiable now it was known. The bird above her head sang an elaborate obbligato into her thoughts. It occurred to her that if her husband had needed her, if he had not left her, if he were not far away, and otherwise occupied, she could not have reached so simple a conclusion. Or, perhaps, the conclusion once reached would have been less simple. But Donald lived his own life. As to her job in Hull, she would give notice. There was nothing unique about being a dispensing chemist, they could replace her. And there were dispensaries everywhere. She could find another job when she wanted to. She had wilfully decided long ago to be ordinary, and she had achieved it, with what advantages it had.

Toby called her from the house. 'We've made some tea, Mother. Will you come?'

She felt their excitement as soon as she sat down with them. A just perceptible tension in the room. She knew them so well they would never, lifelong, be able to keep things from her – or at least they would be able to keep from her the reasons for what they felt, but never the feelings.

'You found something?' she asked.

'Yes,' said Alice. 'Not what we were looking for. Toby found *that.*' She grimaced as Toby flung open the lid of a tin trunk that he had placed on the kitchen table, the other end from the tea things where they sat. It was full of envelopes. He picked up a clutch of them, and held them out to her.

'Just look at them, Ma,' he said. 'She hasn't even opened them, and some of them are postmarked in the seventies!'

Tax returns, tax demands, electoral roll forms, bank statements, buff-envelope letters of every kind – soon they had the table covered with unopened communications, many of them stamped with URGENT and other assorted dire warnings. They began to laugh, awestruck.

'But look . . .' Toby picked up a knife and slit open an envelope at random. It summoned Stella to an interview, which she was to attend without fail, with a local bank manager in Cambridge, on the sixth of September, 1978. He urgently needed to discuss her account with her.

'It won't be funny sorting it all out,' he said. 'What will you do?'

'Most of it will have sorted itself out by now,' said Marian. 'I shan't do anything until the time comes to hand it all over to the solicitors. Close the lid, son. Drink your tea.'

Visiting Stella had become hard. Holding her un-responsive hand, talking into the silence, sounding foolish, knowing that given the possibility of answering such idle remarks Stella's retort would have been crushing, they found now, all three of them found, that they were weighed down with guilt at having ransacked Stella's house, felt as though they had been caught red-handed in some unpardonable act of busybodying. They had not found a living will. They had found other things.

Toby had found that his grandmother was deeply in debt. He had not been able to resist opening, reading, sorting, the contents of the tin trunk. He had hauled it up to his room under the skylights, put up a card table beside the desk to make more sorting space, and worked doggedly through the bills and letters. Stella had spent money steadily, which apparently she did not have. She had multiple bank accounts, which had all slid into over-draft, and then been left dormant. When she earned any money, as far as he could tell, she simply paid it into a new account rather than clearing any of the debt on an old one. It would take him weeks to sort out. He opened incredibly frightening missives, threatening distraint upon goods, proceedings in court, bankruptcy suits, and was appalled at his grandmother's sang-froid in ignoring them. 'Gran, how could you?' he asked the empty room, and then realized since she hadn't opened anything, she hadn't known about it. Had she frustrated them all simply by not reading their letters? Had they all just given up and gone away?

He began a methodical tally, totting up the amounts owing on each account he discovered. He couldn't imagine how she had got away with it. On the face of it she was mortgaged to the eyebrows, and that lamb chop should have been the last step into bankruptcy. Toby was appalled. Like many people who have always had enough money – the careful son of a prosperous and generous father – he was afraid of money, or rather of the lack of it. He understood gradations of wealth easily – could have measured the distance between himself and the senior partner in the stockbroking firm for which he worked in terms of exactly how much after-tax income, exactly how many promotions, it was composed of. Gradations of poverty were unfamiliar territory. He had no idea how little was enough; no idea what it cost to buy a loaf and a tin of beans. He had been doing well; by forty he would be provided for for life.

Or would have been, rather. He had not told his mother or his sister why he could so easily take time out. That he was under a shadow. Someone had been naughty; there was a nasty suspicion of insider dealing, and several people, Toby among them, had been suspended on full pay while a discreet internal enquiry was conducted. Toby's own involvement had been marginal. He had overheard something in the office, and enlisted his current girl-friend. She was no longer current, as a result. Toby had lent her enough to buy a few hundred shares, but she had told her father, who had staked enough to make a difference, to attract attention. None of this would matter had other people in his firm not done the same – other more senior people. Cumulatively they had made a big blip on the charts, and now there was a hue and cry going on. Toby's footprints would be hard to trace. But being nearly sure they couldn't pin anything on him was not the point. He had so blithely got into trouble – sailed over the line into dishonesty without a second's thought. Now he was ashamed of himself. At least he would never do anything like that ever again! But he wasn't in a good position to blow the whistle on others, others senior to himself. He thought he would wait and see what they found out. It was up to them to find out. And meanwhile he could follow the prices, read the *Financial Times*, take a little time to reflect. Be a help to his mother, and sort out the terrible trunk. Twenty minutes of it was enough to convince him his own financial wizardry must come packaged with his father's genes, and have nothing to do with any matrilineal descent from Stella.

While he worked methodically through the piles of paperwork, it occurred to him to wonder about that other line of descent. Stella must have had a little help producing his mother; had his grandfather perhaps been good at money, had a head for figures? He and Stella must have had remarkably little in common, if so. How could she have lived like that? Wasn't she afraid of being found out? But it was he himself who was afraid of being found out.

Alice came to call him for lunch. 'How's it going?' she asked him.

'It's horrendous,' he told her. 'She simply didn't pay her debts, as far as I can see.'

'Unless she paid in cash,' suggested Alice. 'She often had stacks of cash stuffed away somewhere. I saw her pay a gas bill once, over the counter in the Gas Board showroom, in handfuls of crumpled notes.'

'Humm,' said Toby. 'Well, that would explain why she is now laid out under a cover of respectability in the local hospital instead of in a debtor's prison.' He was baffled. The cash economy, beyond the realms of small change, lay outside his province.

'She always *might* have sold a picture,' suggested Alice,

leaning back in a battered cane armchair, and stretching her legs. 'I'm going back to London tonight, if you can spare me. Just till tomorrow. OK? I take it I can leave you parent-sitting for the moment – no duty calls you back to the job as yet?'

'Not yet,' he said. It would be much harder, he realized, to tell his sister what had been happening to him than to tell his mother. Alice was only too ready to think the worst of him.

'Social life?' he asked. He was afraid she would mention Max, that she would be going to see the famous Max. Max was the leader of the quartet Alice played in. He was much older than Alice. He was cold and sarcastic to non-musical people like Toby, who had only met him once and instantly hated him. Alice lived with Max, on and off. And she probably was going to see him, but what she said was, 'This is all taking much longer than I thought it would. I need my viola.'

'Right. We'll cope no doubt. Go and get the thing, and then we'll have to listen to it. And last time I stayed with you you did the same three notes all day. Oh, Lord!'

'The barn,' she said. 'I shall serenade the paintings in the barn.'

'Those paintings,' he said, 'will have to be . . .'

'. . . sorted. Yes. If she dies.'

'When. You mean when.'

'Yes. Meanwhile I suppose we should look for the will thing in there too.'

'See what Mum says.' For they both knew that they were all postponing the barn. That going in there and rifling through things there was a major step, compared to which ransacking every other room in Stella's house was a bagatelle. Stella didn't live in any other room in her house in any way that mattered to her; the studio was the only door that had ever been closed against her grandchildren.

'Toby?' said Alice, standing in the bedroom door, poised to leave. 'Nobody has come looking for you – nobody has rung.'

'Who were you expecting?' He spoke sharply.

'A girlfriend? Someone from work?'

'There's no girlfriend at the moment. And I have some leave owing. I told you.'

'So you did,' she said, disappearing down the stairs.

But it's all very odd, he reflected. Like those fairy tales Mum used to read us when we were children. About getting stolen away. The tiny part of his life that consisted of being Stella's grandson had suddenly ambushed him, and entrapped him. He was lost to his usual world, and could not tell when he would enter it again. And here he was floating, a non-participant – that's why he had invented a role for himself, was busily sorting papers. The real job, as he saw it, was simply being on hand in case his mother needed him. Well, she visibly did need him, them both. But being needed in this passive sense reminded him dimly of playing cricket, of being a catcher in the outfield, waiting for a whizzing ball that never came.

Why think of cricket after all these years? He realized that beyond the bedroom window, beyond the garden hedge, he had heard something without quite registering it. The clunk of ball on bat. Time had been passing. It was the first Saturday in May, after all. They were playing cricket on the village green.

He tipped the lid of the trunk shut, and went out to watch the game.

Marian was alone in the house, writing letters. She was arranging to leave her normal life in abeyance indefinitely. There wasn't much to it, really – the assistant pharmacist could run the shop, would enjoy it, and appreciate the extra money. A neighbour would keep an eye on the house. Not even a cat to arrange for. She had meant it to be a rooted life, a steady and quiet one, but could it really be that floating free was as easy as this? She looked at her watch, and got up to put her coat on. She fished the car-keys out of the pocket, and went out to the front. A man was advancing down the drive.

'Can I help you?' she said, scanning him. Stocky, sixty-something, sharp gaze under bushy eyebrows, dirty hands with broken fingernails, shabby clothes, something heavy in every pocket.

'Shouldn't think so,' he said, marching past her and making for the back door.

'It's locked,' she said to his back. 'Nobody's there.'

He stopped, and said without turning round, 'She's in the barn, then.'

'No,' said Marian, 'in hospital.'

'Shit!' he said. 'Now what?'

'I don't know. I'm on my way to visit.'

'Oh well, then,' he said, turning to stare at her, 'I'll wait. You can ask her. Tell her that Leo came – that I need the money now.'

'My mother owes you money?'

'Yes, she does,' he said. 'That is – she is paying for something in instalments. I've got to have the money, or else . . . Didn't know she had family,' he added. 'Not much in evidence, usually, are you?'

'What is it she is paying for?' asked Marian, angered and cold.

'Just ask her. She can tell you if she wants you to know.'

'I can ask her, but she can't tell me. She has had a stroke, and can't speak.'

'Oh, shit,' he said again. 'I'm sorry, I just assumed . . . I mean, last time it wasn't serious—'

'What wasn't serious?'

'Last time she was in hospital. They only kept her for a day. I wouldn't have mentioned the money, only I thought . . . I don't know what to do.'

'Take yourself off,' suggested Marian.

He didn't move. He looked at Marian strangely – his expression at once wooden-faced and desperate. 'Will she be all right?' he said. 'How bad is it? She'll kill me if I botch her job.'

'She isn't in any state to do that. She may never be again. You need have no fear for your own safety,' said Marian, and saw him wince at that.

He just stood there, in the middle of the drive, rigid. But he knew about some earlier hospitalization that she herself had not been told about. And she could not be sure her mother had not entered some agreement with a shady-looking stranger. She could not be sure of anything about Stella. But her own standards of conduct forbade leaving tradesmen in difficulties, forbade the postponement of debt.

'A hire purchase agreement, you say? Do you have anything in writing?'

'No,' he said. 'It's word of honour.'

'I can advance fifty pounds,' she said, sighing, 'while we get my mother's affairs sorted out. Against a written receipt.' She opened her bag, tore a page from her note-book, and wrote 'Received £50' and watched him sign it.

'Anally retentive old bag, aren't you?' he said, handing it over.

She counted out fifty pounds, in ten pound notes, noting that it left her short and would impose a trip to the cash dispenser on her way home, and cursing herself for a fool and a coward.

'Thank *you*,' he said, still looking at her strangely, thrusting the money into a back pocket. She watched him plod away down the drive. Then she got into her car and drove off towards Cambridge. In the hospital car-park she glanced at the receipt, thinking that she could tell Stella. It would make a thing to say into the oppressive silence. It was signed 'Leo D. Vincey.'

'Shit!' said Marian in her turn, slamming the car door far too hard.

'Mother, is Leonardo da Vinci a personal friend of yours?' Marian asked the supine form under the sheet. 'Is he a disreputable looking heavy in shabby clothes, not above demanding money with menaces, from whom you are buying an unspecified object on instalments?' She got no audible answer, but an expression – a sort of jerk to the right side of Stella's slack mouth occurred, which might have been a reaction to Marian's message, and might have been coincidence.

'I find it hard to tell, with you,' Marian went on. 'I wouldn't have thought he could be anything but a sponger. He couldn't be a blackmailer – what could he allege about you that you wouldn't be indifferent to being known? And while we're talking like this, Mother, I'd like to know something – anything – about my father. I've been wondering about him. We lost him in the war, you said – you didn't say how. You didn't give me his surname – I am an obvious bastard? I said once, perhaps I got my liking for tidiness, and ability at arithmetic from him, and you said no, he wasn't an educated man, and he wasn't tidy. Was he an artist? I asked you once, and you said no, he knew nothing about art at all, but he had a good eye. A good eye for tits and a bum, as well, come to that, you said. You said once we couldn't go back somewhere, because of him – was it Concarneau? Was it Italy? Was it Spain? Was it where the beaches were, was it him who held me in his buttoned coat all night long while we waited for a tide to fall back? Where was that? That cave? You must realize that it isn't much to know about a father. It isn't enough, it leaves me not knowing enough. There he is, running in my bloodstream and in my children's bloodstream, and we don't know a thing. Those forms – you know those forms, Mother, that they make you fill out when you're ill in some way, or on research projects – *What did your parents die of? Has anyone in your family had cancer?* We have to tick 'unknown' every time. Why didn't you tell me, why didn't I ask you before? I should have battered it out of you while you could still speak. And now what?'

She shrugged helplessly, and reached out for her mother's hand. And thought that her mother had squeezed hers, for she felt the unfurled fingers tighten in a passing spasm that might not have been an accident.

'This is taking too long, Mother.' She said it sorrowfully, and saw what she would have sworn was understanding and agreement pass across the less frozen side of her mother's face. 'We have to deal with things. I have to read your papers, pay your bills, try to get a deed of attorney. We might have to sell your house; I'll try not to, but we might. We shall have to clear things out of it. Oh, Mother, it feels terrible – a terrible thing to do. You would so have hated it, wouldn't you? I'm so at sea in your life, I'm going to make horrible mistakes. Give me permission – blink at me if I may do whatever I think needs doing – can you?' Stella slowly closed her eyes, and slowly opened them.

To the sister, who stopped her on the way out, and offered a cup of tea when she saw Marian's face frozen with strain, Marian said, no, she hadn't found a nursing home. 'She can be in her own home. I shall look after her.'

The sister ushered her into the ward office, and offered a chair. 'Would your mother have wanted that, Mrs Easton? Only many of our patients are desperately anxious *not* to burden their families, not to disrupt younger lives. Perhaps for you to give up your home and move in and nurse her isn't what she would want . . .'

'It's what I want,' said Marian. 'She can't always have her own way.'

A cup of red-brown tea in a thick white cup and saucer had appeared before her. She sipped it, unwillingly.

'Is it money?' the sister asked. Her tone was of gentle professional concern. In a minute she would offer an interview with a social worker, and a means test. 'Is there a problem paying for residential care?'

'No it's *not* money!' Marian snapped at her. 'It's love.'

And the word once spoken, like a bird let out of a box, flew away abruptly leaving silence and stillness behind.

'We'll keep her a few days more, while you think about it,' said the sister.

There aren't many hills in Cambridgeshire – none that would count as hillocks in Yorkshire. But one of the few gentle rises was on the road between the hospital and Stella's house. Marian drove herself home and stopped the car on the crest. The towers of a cement works edged into view on the right of the road; on the left a stretch of England lay in sight, an unremarkable prospect, without any particular beauties – just gently undulant green fields, patched with scraps of woodland, and here and there a church tower. The season was poised now between spring and summer. A dusting of bright yellow lay across acres of rape, just now gone over, and nearer was a field of flax that looked like water under a grey sky, with the wind trailing swathes of green through it, rocking its fragile flowers. It isn't that flat land is less beautiful, Marian thought, surprised, it's just that it's harder to get a view of it.

It occurred to her as she started the car that there was some kind of parallel. These hard days were like the gentle upswing of the minimal hill she was on – giving a view, letting her see what her life and her mother's life had been like, which while being lived went unconsidered.

But it had been true, the word she never spoke to Stella. If she hadn't loved her mother – if she had been able to manage the casual indifference, the dismissive mentions, the patronizing got-to-humour-the-poor-old-boot attitudes of other people in adult life to their parents – she would have been free. She wouldn't have needed to strive so bitterly to be different. To be the shadow to every light in her mother's life, the light to every shadow. To be practical, to be tidy, to be dutiful, to be attentive and kind, to choose a place and live in it, to stay put lifelong, to have no interest in art, no opinions on anything intellectual – it was loving her mother that had laid these heavy shackles on her, as though she could by being at the opposite pole in some way pay her mother's unpaid debts, make up her mother's shortfall, pay her mother's unpaid tribute to convention, to normal conduct, to uncontroversial judgement about how to live.

This insight came to her with a guilty start, like a recollection of a duty neglected. Something she didn't want to know, but ought already to have known – hadn't Stella once told her that an unconsidered life was not worth living?

What needed considering now, of course, was nursing Stella. A hospital bed would be needed; it was backbreaking work to turn, wash, feed a patient on a normal one.

'Where will we get one?' asked Alice. A severely practical discussion was in flow around the kitchen table.

'We hire it from the Red Cross, I think,' said Marian.

'And we put it – where?' asked Toby.

They turned over the possibilities together. Not the kitchen. The bedrooms were small, and the cramped little stair with a wind in it was likely to make bed-hauling impossible. The living room was needed for the minimal comfort of whoever was living in and nursing, and in any case was rather gloomy, facing the screen of trees, and getting no sun.

'The barn,' said Alice. 'It has to be the barn.'

'Brace yourself, mother,' said Toby. 'It has to be the barn, and we have to turn it out. We have to, sometime.'

'Yes,' said Marian. 'We do.'

Toby opened the barn door briskly, and the three of them stood together on the threshold. A threefold unspoken reluctance overcame them. Marian remembered herself small – with a grazed knee, or with impossible homework, standing at some quite different door. Toby remembered pushing Alice ahead of him, starving hungry, wanting to ask when dinner . . . Alice remembered her grandmother, so kind, so permissive in every other room in the world, so ferocious and self-defended in this one – there rang in the silence for all of them the familiar autocratic voice saying, 'Get *out*!'

Here above all was where Stella had lived; here her absence loomed immanently, and it seemed ignoble and dangerous to take advantage of it. Toby was boldest, and unfroze first. They moved into the room. And the swiftest look around convinced them. The barn had two large wagon-doors, filled in as windows, facing each other amidships. One was heavily screened in coarse calico – that one faced south, and could be uncurtained to admit some cheerful light. The workbench on the wall against the house had an old butler's sink plumbed in – for washing those brushes? – it would be useful. You could easily move the easels, and shift away the ramshackle shelving, with paints, tins and bottles, encrusted pallets, stacks of frame mouldings. There was a little cast iron stove that looked capable of enough warmth if kept fuelled. There was room for a bed, and a chair, and the clobber of a sick room, or at least there would be if the paintings were removed.

The paintings were stacked on edge, leaning face down against each other, dozens and dozens deep. Long lines of the tilted boards backed away from the walls across the floor space.

'We could move them up there – perhaps?' said Alice uncertainly. She pointed to the hay floor, a platform halfway up the walls, which covered some third of the barn. It was inaccessible, except by a steep fixed ladder. Toby scrambled up. 'There's room up here,' he reported. 'Quite a lot would go here, if we pack them tightly.'

Alice said, 'We ought to sort them. We ought to see if there's any kind of rhyme or reason in how they are stacked, and we ought to keep them together as they are if there is. Any system, that is.'

'No-one's ever going to care, sib,' said Toby from on high. 'They'll all finish up being lugged into the orchard and burnt.'

'They're worthless, you mean? Gran's entire life's work, and all you can think is burn it?' Standing below him in the middle of the floor, Alice was suddenly screaming at Toby.

'Well, if they were worth anything, she would have been able to sell them . . .'

'Everything comes down to money for you, doesn't it? The great god money, the measure of all things! Just as well you're so sodding good at earning it, because there's fuck all else you'd be good for!'

He had opened his mouth to scream back at her, the old familiar adolescent in-fighting pulling him like a needle in a record track, when his adult self supervened. Why was Alice picking on him like that? Answer: she was unhappy. There she was, standing below him full of rage and misery, and it had nothing to do with him. It probably didn't have much to do with Stella, either, it was probably about Max.

'Not here, Alice, not now,' he said. 'Bitch at me some other time. Let's get going. Change places with me, Alice – those things will be heavy. I'll heave them up to you, and you can stack them, and Mother can watch and wait.' One by one Toby turned canvases over and passed them up to Alice. Landscapes, and flower paintings, worked in thick paint, in bright solid colours. They might have been recognizable, Marian supposed – this procession of scenes must contain the palimpsest record of her headlong, disrupted childhood, she should have been able to name the places, if she could see as Stella saw. Instead she could name the feeling in which they were eloquent, urgent – that sense of displacement—

'What are they, anyway?' Toby asked, pausing for breath.

'What do you mean, what are they?' said Alice. 'They're all of different things.'

'I mean, are they impressionist, expressionist, colourist, fauve?'

'No good asking me. Mother? You must know something about these.'

'No, I don't,' said Marian. 'Stellist – that's what they are. I don't know anything about them; I wouldn't look, I wouldn't listen, I wouldn't know, I was afraid of it – of them – I wanted to be useful.'

Her tone of voice brought Alice scrambling down the ladder to her side.

'You were, to us. You were all the world to us,' she said, squeezing her mother's hand. Marian smiled at her. Though she had heard the necessary past tense.

'But what would be useful now . . .' she admitted.

She had been staring for some time at the canvas

standing on the easel in the middle of the room. It was a
new one; covered with a smooth grey-blue wash, darker
below, lighter above. Its greyness and emptiness appalled
her, as though instead of it giving way to Stella's bright
vision, it had captured and invaded Stella, emptied her of
sight and sound . . . Marian was swaying on her feet, she
couldn't control her weariness – if she sat down she would
fall asleep. As though thinking were work, as though
feeling could drag you down like hard labour . . .

'Hey, Ma!' Toby was saying. 'Ma, look at this! Gran
kept something of yours. You must have done this.'

He was holding out to her a little picture, done on cardboard. It showed three big boats and a little one sailing
past a lighthouse on a chalky-grey sea. Fishes swam along
the lower margin. A line of houses endways up bordered
the scene on the left.

'No,' said Marian, 'not mine.'

'You wouldn't remember,' her son told her. 'It isn't
Gran's, anyway; all hers are initialled. Hang on; look at
this.'

He held up for her, back facing, a canvas on which was
scrawled in chalk, 'For Marian.' Nothing else. Then he
turned it over, and set it up against the canvas already there
on the easel.

It showed a man sitting naked in a wooden chair,
indoors, in front of an open window. He was looking into
the room, and the cast of the light composed him of
shadow, brightly aureoled. His hands lay slackly in his lap,
preserving modesty, though they were the centre of the
picture and drew the eye. Large hands, roughened, with
broken grimy nails, held stiffly as though unused to lying
at rest. His clothes lay tumbled at his feet, on bare floorboards on which, right at the edge, the familiar 'S.H.' had
been painted in grey. He looked both muscular and thin,

wiry, one might have said. And under the shade of his thick dishevelled hair his eyes stared out at them, unreadable, watchful, dark. Through the window behind him a patch of blue, a section of wall, a sketched-in schematic boat, and bright sky.

'Who is it?' said Alice, softly.

'I don't know, I don't know,' Marian said.

Faintly, in the house, the phone began to ring.

It was Alice who took the call, and brought the message back into the barn. Stella's dying was done.

There was a lot to do, then. A funeral to arrange. Telling Stella's friends seemed an impossible task – they couldn't find her address book, and Marian didn't necessarily know who they were. Toby put an announcement in *The Times* and the *Telegraph*. Marian found a funeral director in the Yellow Pages. He was a quiet, soft-spoken, courteous man to whom it seemed possible to leave decisions. Neighbours came calling. 'I didn't know her well, but . . .' Nobody had known Stella well, but they were very sorry. It was, evidently, a decent place. They were sorry they hadn't known her better; 'She was always so busy – you have to hand it to her,' said the woman immediately the other side of the thick holly hedge. 'I admired her for that.'

Marian and her children were cast adrift. The routine they had set up, each of them visiting every day, shopping and cooking for each other, was suspended. And then there were surprises. Toby went across to the village shop and bought copies of *The Times* and the *Telegraph* to check the notices he had put in, and later, Alice, flicking idly through *The Times,* found an obituary notice of Stella. It had not crossed anyone's mind to look for such a thing.

'Mum! Toby!' she called. 'Come and look at this!' They spread out the paper on the table, and pored over it together.

> Stella Harnaker, painter, died in Cambridge on May 30th, aged 84. She was born in Lewes, Sussex, on December 16, 1911.
>
> Stella Harnaker trained at the Putney School of Art from 1928-31. She worked briefly in Florence, before settling for some years in St Ives, Cornwall, where she was a prominent figure in the St Ives Society of Artists. She painted landscapes and still life, in a broadly post-impressionist style. She was clearly influenced during the war years by the work of the modernists who had settled in St Ives. But she was among those who left the Penwith Society, founded by Barbara Hepworth and Ben Nicholson, shortly after it was formed, and strongly supported the traditionalist faction in the increasingly divided St Ives artists' community. After the war, Harnaker reverted to her pre-war style, and worked for some years abroad, before returning to live in Brighton, and then near Cambridge. In spite of the obscurity of her later years, Harnaker's St Ives period works are of interest, dramatizing as they do the conflict between the modernist and the traditionalist vision, and she has always had a following among her fellow painters. She is survived by a daughter.

'Golly,' said Toby. 'Did you know all this, Ma?'

And Marian said, bleakly, 'No, I didn't know all this. I did know about the obscurity. I suppose I survived her.'

Alice said, 'So that's where your beaches are, Mum.'

Toby put an arm round Marian's shoulder, and squeezed her. 'We'll go there,' he said. 'I'll take you there, and you can see your beaches again. Places change, but I don't suppose beaches do, much. We'll go. OK?'

'We've got a funeral first,' said Marian.

It was on a bleak, rain-swept afternoon, at the crematorium on the main road. It had seemed somehow unseemly to impose church on her in death, which they never would have dared to do in life. And yet even in a crematorium chapel one has to do *something*; the undertaker had arranged a chaplain. And there were people there. There had been one or two phone calls to the house, enquiring for time and place, but there were more than one or two strangers among the mourners. And, Marian noticed at once, the mourners included Leonardo da Vinci, tidied up, and complete with black armband and black tie. Brief though it was, the service caused Marian pain, for it included an injunction to look at the flowers, and see that they were all right, and a breathtakingly perverse and ignorant declaration that, 'The Lord is my shepherd, I shall have everything I want.'

'It's bad enough', Marian reflected bitterly, 'to be left alone in the world, to be an orphan, without being made to feel that one is a solitary survivor of civilization itself, of one's language, of one's religion. That one is living now among barbarians.'

The chaplain said, standing on a sort of stand that was ashamed to be openly a pulpit, that he understood very well that Stella had not believed in God, and that many of the people gathered here today in her memory likewise did not believe in God. 'Never mind,' he said, 'God believes in you.' It had always seemed to him, he added, that God must be particularly fond of creative people, being himself a creator. Stella would be safe in his hands; perhaps now and then – he liked to think so – God let a dead painter do the sunset for the day. Sometimes he was sure it was from the hand of Turner; sometimes it might be a Japanese printmaker's work, sometimes it was Constable. He would look out for Stella as he drove himself home on winter evenings.

Marian thanked the chaplain sweetly, and invited everyone who wished to come back to the house. 'But, dear Jesus!' she muttered to Alice, who was looking inappropriately beautiful, black suited her so much, 'What would your grandmother have said to that!'

Alice laughed. 'I hope there's enough to eat, mum,' she said anxiously. 'I wasn't expecting many people.'

'It doesn't matter so much at teatime,' Marian said.

'Well, if they knew Gran they won't be expecting much,' said Toby.

Perhaps they weren't; they didn't stay long. Most of them were neighbours; one was an old friend of Stella's from art school days, who came in a taxi all the way from London, a frail old lady with a stick, and whose taxi was lurking outside, making her tea lethally expensive. 'You're going to miss her very much,' she said to Alice. 'There never was anybody like her. Nobody at all.'

'Were you a friend of Gran's? Did you like her?' Alice asked boldly, horrifying Marian who was standing beside them, offering a plate of biscuits.

'No,' said the old lady, surprisingly. 'No, I didn't. But I thought she was wonderful.' Then into the silence she added, 'Candid – like you, young woman.' And then 'I wonder who wrote that obit. It wasn't very generous, was it? Perhaps Violet Garthen . . .'

'We don't know, I'm afraid,' said Alice.

It's an uneasy sort of gathering at best, a funeral tea. Nobody knows whether they are supposed to be enjoying themselves. Anecdotes about Stella probably better left untold hovered in the air. People began to depart.

Marian looked round at an empty living room. She sat down in the nearest armchair.

'That's that, then,' she said to Alice. 'Leave the clearing, love, we can do it later. Did that Leonardo person go without making a nuisance of himself?'

'Not exactly,' said Toby. 'He's just gone out to his car to fetch his things.'

'What things?' asked Marian in alarm.

Toby gestured towards the kitchen door behind him, and Leonardo came in, bearing a bulging duffel bag in one hand, and a bottle of whisky in the other. 'Let's stop pissing about with tea, and have a proper drink,' he said. 'I'm sure you need it as much as I do.'

All three Eastons were staring, not so much at him, as at his bag, dumped on the kitchen table.

'I've come to stay for a few days,' he said. 'I reckoned you were going to need some help.'

'We can manage—' Marian began. She was too tired to sound angry. What was the matter with her? Why was she always tired?

'Sorting paintings,' he said. 'You're going to need help with that.'

'Yes, we are,' said Alice. 'We do. Come and look.' She led him through to the barn. He was still carrying his bottle. Toby and Marian followed. What faced them at once was the large easel, bearing the grey, empty canvas, and the small picture leaning in front of it.

'Who's that?' Alice asked. 'Do you know who that is?'

'Yes, I do,' he said. 'It's rather good, isn't it? Wouldn't mind having done that. I've lost his name for the moment – I'll get it in a minute, but I can tell you who he is. He missed the boat.'

'What boat?' Alice asked.

'A lifeboat,' said Leo, 'what do you know about lifeboats?'

'Nothing much,' said Toby.

'Pour me a drink and I'll tell you about it.'

They settled Leo down at the kitchen table with a glass of his own whisky.

'Have you ever lived in a place with a lifeboat station?' he asked them.

'There might have been one at Brighton,' said Marian. 'I lived there for a bit. I can't remember.'

'If you haven't you might not get it,' said Leo. 'There's even people thinking it's some sort of government service, like it is in other countries. It's all done by the coastguard in America, I've been told. Paid for out of taxes.'

'Well, someone must pay for it, here,' said Toby. 'Isn't it a charity?'

'The boats and the gear are paid for out of charity, but the men are all volunteers. They've all got other jobs; but when the rocket goes up they down tools, leave meals half-eaten, and customers standing, and they get the hell down to the wharf. Unpaid. Well, the coxswain gets a pittance over the winter months, but nobody does it for money. They were all fishermen then, of course. Fishing was the town's living.'

'When was then?' asked Alice.

'Before the war. Well, the lifeboat continues to the present day, of course, but I'm telling you about thirty-nine.'

'Was my mother there, then?' asked Marian.

'Yes. The fishing was declining already, and the artists could get cheap lodging, and have old sail-lofts and boat-sheds for studios. The town had artists like rabbits in a warren. I was there myself, come to that, though I was only a nipper.'

'But there weren't any artists in the lifeboat?'

'God, no. I don't know how to explain . . . Two things. First, it's fiercely contested. It's a signal honour to be regular crew. The young men can't hold their heads up till they've held a jacket for a spell. It makes a man of you; and there's only eight in a crew − not enough to go round for the natives, back then, and none to spare for others. Second thing, it's bloody dangerous. Well, they have better boats now, I grant you; but even so. The open Atlantic beats right up to the doors of the town, and that's a wicked coast right up to the Bristol Channel.'

Toby reached out and picked up the whisky bottle, and refilled Leo's glass.

'And there's a special problem over the lifeboat, there. There's got to be one. And it's got to put out into the high seas, but low tide goes right out of the harbour. So half the time the boat can't launch into water, but it's got to be dragged across the sands on a trolley, and there's a limit to how big a boat you can manage on a trolley. They have a submersible tractor now, but it used to take eighty men on two ropes, going into the water to their chins, before she could be floated off.'

'So how big was it? What was it like?' asked Toby. He had done some sailing, in San Franciso Bay. Not that he was an expert—'

'I don't know how big. I was only a nipper, creeping out of bed wrapped in a raincoat to watch. There was a wind out of hell blowing, and I got soaked to the skin. My mother gave me a leathering when she caught me, for risking my health . . . The significant thing about that boat was she was a self-righting boat. So she only drew two foot something below the water-line. She was a replacement boat, just like the one they had lost the year before, and there's no way that wasn't in everyone's mind.'

'What had happened to the other boat?'

'She capsized. No loss of life, that time, just gold medals all round. But everyone knew how easily that other boat had gone over—'

'You didn't say why people do it,' Marian prompted him. Of course, she had been reconsidering the great Leonardo during this exposition. His funeral black made him look more like a dignitary than a plumber. Her line of sight brought into view the receipt he had given her, propped against a plate on the dresser.

'Why do they do it?' he said. 'It's fear of drowning, I think. Horror at the thought. Next time it might be one of them. Ironic, really, when you think that a good way of keeping safe from drowning would be to keep on dry land in hurricanes. Religion might have something to do with it too; they're all Methodists, if they aren't Salvationists. They think they are in the hands of God.'

'So that day in thirty-nine – what happened?'

'Night. It was night. And a fearful storm. The rockets went up at two in the morning. The tide was out. Everyone was out on the wharf – the men to give a hand to launch her, and the women all standing at the top of the slip, wailing and calling out to their men – "think what you've got at home," and "you aren't going," and – well, you can imagine. And it came clear she was short-handed. There was a bit of argy-bargy then. One man got into the boat and then changed his mind about it, and gave his life-jacket back. The coxswain said, "I want somebody to go." And a man called William Freeman said, "All right, I'll go. I'll do."

'The coxswain said, "All right, you'll do." I heard him say it, I was hanging on a lamppost right there where they were passing. So Freeman put the jacket on and went in the boat. That's what happened, basically. The coxswain was short-handed, and he took volunteers. Well, they got her afloat. And that boat no sooner got out of the bay than she went over. She capsized three times, and each time she righted again there were fewer men in her, till there was only Freeman left. He was still in the boat when she hit the rocks on the further side of the bay, and he somehow got through the surf and up the cliff, and to a farmhouse. The telephone lines were down in the storm, and the farmer had to ride to Hayle to get the news through. It was seven in the morning before they knew it at St Ives. It left twenty-one widows and orphans. Someone gone out of every web of family in the town.'

'God help us, what a terrible story,' said Marian.

'Yes, it was,' Leo said. 'Inquests and funerals, and waiting for the sea to deliver the dead . . . for a few days there was talk of it having been all for nothing; of the boat having been launched on a false alarm. But by and by there was wreckage washed up in the coves along the shore to Pendeen. And bodies. More lives lost. Believe me, that wasn't a good time to be someone who had missed the boat.

'It didn't die down, you see. There was hell to pay. All those funerals, one after another, thousands of people packing the chapels, coming from all over Cornwall and beyond. Everyone counting on their fingers, and saying well I saw that one down there at the launch, and I didn't see that one. Where was he, where were you, where was I? Hell to pay. Now the second cox, he didn't hear the rocket. He was moved into a council house somewhere back along, away from the sea. He'd lost his father, and he'd lost his younger brother, and he was distracted. Others living up where he lived hadn't heard it either, what with the wind. The man that got into the boat and got out of it again, and gave his jacket away to Willy Freeman, he paid for that for the rest of his life, all but. People never got square with him about that. And there had been terrible confusion in the dark, and you couldn't hardly hear yourself speak. And people shaking in their boots if they were honest, going, or not going with her. But let's just say that your man there – Thomas Tremorvah, that's who it is – was one who might have been down there, and offering to go, and he wasn't. He hadn't heard the rocket no more than Thomas Cocking junior, he said. But he would have heard it if he'd been where he should have been. Edgar Basset lived right near him, and Basset heard it and went down to the boat to be drowned with the others. But somehow Tommy Tremorvah missed it.'

'So why did Gran give the picture of Thomas Tremorvah to Mum?' said Alice. They were still sitting in the kitchen, all four of them, making a scratch supper of the remains of the funeral tea.

'Did she? In so many words?'

'It says "For Marian" on the back,' Toby told him.

'Well, then, it's hers,' said Leo.

'But they're all hers, anyway,' said Toby. They had found a dead will, if not a living one.

'And what can I do with them?' asked Marian. 'Of course I shall keep some but—'

'There are impractically many,' Leo completed the sentence for her. 'Well, look, I've got a day to spare. I'm on my way up north, and not expected till Friday. I'll put them in two stacks for you. Saleable and unsaleable. You need to get in cahoots with a gallery and put the saleable ones on the market a few at a time. I can probably find you someone . . .'

Alice had got up, and fetched the teapot from the dresser, moving towards the kettle on the side. As she did so something was dislodged and fluttered to the floor. She put the teapot down and picked it up. She frowned. Then she slammed the paper down on the table, and said, 'What the hell is this? Is this something to do with you?'

It was the receipt signed 'Leo D. Vincey.'

Toby picked it up and stared at it. Marian winced.

'Is that something to do with you?' Alice demanded. 'What's going on? That can't be your name!'

'It is almost,' said Leo, grinning at her. 'Leonard Vincey. And my middle name is Derek.'

'But what are you doing?' said Alice at him, through clenched teeth. 'What's going on? Are you positively *trying* to get under my mother's skin? Why? Is it some sort of joke you're playing at? Does it hugely amuse you to get people to misjudge you? You're a sort of self-appointed touchstone for other people's snobberies – is that it? How dare you?'

By now she was shouting at him, and Toby moved round the table, put his arms round her, holding her from behind, and said, 'Alice, don't!'

'I won't have people sending up my mother,' said Alice, in a suddenly small quavering tone.

'I'm so sorry,' Marian said to Leo, anachronistically taking responsibility for what her daughter said. 'Of course we're all tired and overwrought . . .'

'I didn't do it on the day of the funeral,' said Leo, looking at Alice. 'It's an old note. More than a week old.' She wriggled out of Toby's grasp, and sat down facing him.

'So who are you, really?' she said, grimly.

He cocked his head, looking at her intently, inter-rogatively. 'What do you want to know?' he asked.

'One minute you're talking like a tribal fisherman, and the next you're talking like an art dealer.'

'I was a fisherman; likely to be. Then Falmouth Art College, and the world my oyster. That sort of thing.'

'Tell us how you did it,' said Alice.

Leo's face showed a brief passage of emotion, quickly covered up. 'Stella,' he said, 'your bloody grandmother, gave me a box of pastels.'

'That did it?' said Toby. 'She never gave either of us such a thing.'

'It was a great big box,' said Leo. 'A wooden box in two tiers. Straight from Switzerland. Unopened. I can still remember slitting the paper bands that sealed it. I held my breath, and I ran my fingernail along the tiny groove where the paper crossed the edges of the lid and the box. And inside it had eighty-eight colours, all untouched. Every one three inches long, arranged in a marching rainbow. Glorious. There were little brass butterfly hinges on the back of the box, and a red elastic ribbon to hold your sketchbook inside the lid. I would have killed for that box, but I didn't have to. Stella gave it to me.'

'Why?' asked Marian. 'Why did she give it to you?'

'She saw me trying to draw. I had brown paper, rough side up, and a jamjar with chalks she threw away. Little nibs and angles, the worn down ends that got too small to hold. I scrabbled for them in her waste-basket, and got a few colours together. She saw me. I was off school a lot that year, my chest was bad. When I felt poorly my mother sent me to sit in the garden under Stella's window.'

'When was this? How old were you, Leo?'

'Must've been twelve or so. I went mad when I saw those colours. She said she'd spoilt me. She said I was better using dusty little butt-ends.'

'That sounds more like Gran,' said Toby, wryly.

'Yes. She was a good teacher if you could withstand the brutal language.'

'Stella taught you, Leo?' said Marian, wonderingly. All her life she could never remember Stella having a pupil.

'My mother got lessons for me,' he said. 'Stella rented a room to work in – a sail-loft that belonged to my family. When she couldn't stump up the rent my mother took lessons for me in lieu.'

'You've no idea how strange that sounds to us, Leo,' said Alice. 'All the time we knew Gran she threw a fit if anyone came near her when she was working.'

'St Ives was full of that kind of barter,' he said. 'It was full of artists, and they hadn't tuppence to their names sometimes. The locals took paintings or lessons in payment of bad debts. There are probably more good paintings in modest houses in St Ives than anywhere else in England. And bad ones, too, of course. Look, I'm knackered, I need to go to bed. Where am I sleeping?'

Both children glanced at Marian. But she had lost her urge to get rid of Leo. 'The back spare room,' she said. 'I'll share with Alice.'

In the middle of the night Marian eased herself out of bed, moving quietly so as not to disturb Alice in the other bed. Alice was tossing and murmuring, in the grip of some unquiet dream. Marian went barefoot to the kitchen for a glass of water. Leo in a threadbare dressing-gown was rocking himself gently in the wooden rocking-chair, a whisky tumbler half full in his hand.

She sat down opposite him, and he reached out and whiskied her water.

'There's something eating that daughter of yours,' he observed. 'Something serious.'

'Yes. I don't know what. She'll tell me when she wants me to know. I can't think why she should take it out on you.'

'My age? Available father-figure? Real father gone missing?'

'In America. These ten years past.'

'Ah.'

'I suppose you don't know why Tremorvah missed that boat?' she asked.

'I don't, I'm afraid. I don't know where he was, and I don't know why,' Leo said. 'But then I don't know a lot of things. I used to hang around my dad and his friends, give a hand mending nets, and keep my ears open; or I'd help my mother pin sheets out to dry on the Island, and listen to the women, but it didn't cover everything. For example, I didn't know Stella had ever painted Tremorvah. I didn't know she knew him.'

'Wasn't it usual to paint local people?'

'Character portraits, yes. Folksy studies of the wenches gutting fish – that sort of thing. But—'

The striking, defended nudity of the man in the picture hung unmentioned between them. Marian shivered; her bare feet were freezing on the tiled floor.

'Go back to bed,' suggested Leo. 'Why don't you? I often can't sleep. This is my thinking time.'

Something interesting was gradually emerging from Leo's efforts in the barn. Marian wandered in to bring him some coffee. Alice had made the coffee, and filled the row of mugs. She needed coffee all day long, drinking it as a chain-smoker smokes. The sound of her practice session filled the house, grinding a rough zigzag of sound like a growling dog confined upstairs. But the barn was quiet. The easel still carried the canvas with the two zones of grey-blue ground, and the portrait of Thomas Tremorvah propped in front. Leo had simply placed canvases, face out instead of face in, in two groups, one each end of the barn.

At the far end a patchwork of sombre colour faced Marian – an almost lurid flower garden of blooms, blurry leaves, coloured shadows, highlit petals. A closer look revealed that some of the coloured patches were actually landscape – swelling fields, dark woods, black barns – but oddly, they were not really that different from the flower paintings. There was, Marian thought, a kind of gloomy fury in them, a fury of brush-strokes, a fury of the light. In one or two she recognized the subject – a church and field she had walked past going to school in France, a peasant chair that had stood under a fig tree somewhere in Italy. But though Marian remembered sunlight, the paintings had been done in black weather.

They were all initialled and dated, and Leo was putting them into a rough chronology. Gradually the murky colours became brighter, gaudier, raw. The style moved towards abstraction – or did it just become vaguer? Almost as though the painter had averted her eyes . . . Marian had a sharp and curious sense that the paintings did not play fair by the subject. As though the pictures formed a sort of complaint against the world, as though the subject had been *worked up* into a painting, as though seeing were an act of confrontation, an act of anger, of existential rage. It was perfectly clear why these paintings had not sold – who would want such disturbing things on living-room walls?

At the other end of the barn were far fewer pictures, and they were quite different – to Marian's eye they might have been by a different hand. They were cool paintings, done on a white ground, shapes in grey line, and partly filled in with colour, as though they were half finished. Outlines of boats in a harbour, quays, lighthouses. Outlines of roofscape, higgledy-piggledy, with the sea beyond. Many of them were painted through a window, with casement and white curtains offering a broken and irregular frame to a view of part things – part of two boats, half a sail, half a man leaning his weight on a rope. Low headlands ran out from the right of those paintings which had a horizon visible. A lighthouse on a pyramid of offshore rock recurred, as did a green rocky hill tipped with a little chapel. They were all only partly coloured, but what colours they had were bright, flat and uniform. And they were calm. They radiated calm; as though seen with the transcendent radiance of memory. As though painting were a kind of expressive dreaming.

'These are the saleable ones,' said Leo, watching her.

'But these are what one would keep,' said Marian.

'Ah,' he said. 'And then there are these.' He was showing her the child's pictures on cardboard, that Toby had thought she might have done herself. 'Stella didn't do these – she must have bought them. And in view of what she used to say about the artist, that's a bit rich. But there you are, she's got three Alfred Wallises. Just one would pay me what Stella owed me. OK?'

'Leo, how much did she owe you?' asked Marian.

'Ten thousand pounds,' he said. 'Look, I'm seeing a friend this afternoon. I'll finish this job for you tomorrow. Right?'

Marian was sitting in the garden, thinking. Mostly she was thinking about Donald, but also about Stella. Grieving, she was finding, is intransitive; its objects coalesce, it becomes a feeling about itself. Donald had hated Stella, but grief did not choose between them as life had necessarily done. And Marian had gradually swung round between them, like the slowly rotating beat of the Science Museum's pendulum, at first taking Donald's part, wonderful Donald, of whom her dragon mother would take no notice, for whom she would not stop painting, to whom she would barely talk. This hostile behaviour

culminated disastrously with Stella's desertion of the
wedding breakfast, to the scandal of Donald's family, so
that Marian was doomed to the silent sympathy of all her
future in-laws, as though Donald had married a social
misfit of some kind.

Only very slowly had it become apparent to Marian
what Stella's crime had been. Only when other people
committed it likewise, as of course they did, by and by.
Donald liked to be the centre of attention. He liked to be
the cleverest person in the room. Gradually their circle of
acquaintance narrowed to exclude people at whose tables,
round whose firesides, one found eminent guests, pro-
fessors, famous musicians, writers. In the light of this later
knowledge Donald's positive detestation of his mother-
in-law appeared differently. She was only a very glaring
example. There had been a warning not taken, because
not taken in. Blaming Stella, when one was blind with
love, had been easier. That Donald was eminent in his
own field – he was a popular scientist whose books were
very well known – had not assuaged his thirst for attention. That he knew nothing whatever about art did not
impede his adverse judgement of Stella's paintings. Marian
had thought innocently at first that Donald just did not
like them – the ones he had seen, that is – as that early
boyfriend of hers had not liked them. Later she had known
that he could not like any painting that had not been
acclaimed as a masterpiece by an accredited authority.

She had come to think very badly of Donald, though
not to stop loving him. His posturing, his outraged vanity,
could be encompassed in affectionate amusement.
But only an unfailing wellspring of unqualified admiration
– only *deference* would do for him; and he had found it
elsewhere. She had stopped laughing then. His desertion
was not funny, and the loneliness it left her with was

hateful, and unfair. Above all unfair. He had left her for being unable to offer something he was not entitled to expect – something rationed in this hard world, and of which he had had more than his share. You would need to be stupid, or of very limited social horizons, to take Donald at his own estimation. He had left Marian for not being stupid.

Or so she had thought at the time. But perhaps it had more to do with sex. Marian's colleague Susan had told her decisively that when marriages hit trouble it was always sex at the root of it. Simplistic though that sounded, it might, Marian supposed, be right. She didn't know. Her experience of her own sexuality was uncannily like a struggle with an intricate machine, say a computer or a video recorder, delivered without a manual. It had proved possible to make it perform its basic functions – she had, after all, conceived and delivered two children – but it had never been possible to make it perform the fancier functions it was supposed to be capable of, it had never been possible to connect it to happiness. Was that why Donald had left? Had he basically got fed up with fruitless struggles with the tuning? He lived now in considerable prosperity in California, with a much younger woman. Yet whenever Marian thought of him, needed him, she called him 'poor Donald' to herself.

But Marian did not need Donald now. Just Stella. Yet, she knew very well, had Stella been alive she would have been painting, leaving Marian to her own devices. So Marian would have been doing exactly what she was doing now, sitting alone under a garden tree, her thoughts drifting. Surely then it should be possible to hold still, and feel no difference – to feel the world the same. Subtract the moments of attention her mother would have given her – those few – and very little was in any way changed.

But everything was changed. Marian felt like a tree when a great branch was down – unbalanced, straining to cracking point in the lightest breeze. Her whole knowledge of herself had been knowing herself unlike her mother; they had lived like adjacent counties on the map – each inch of territory divided by a boundary so that nothing was in both places, everything was coloured differently, and nothing that Stella was, was Marian. And now the line was gone and the colours were running together, and there was no knowing where she was. Or who. Except that she was no-one's daughter. The whole branching and flourishing daughterliness of her life was torn away and lay broken and dying in the crushed grasses at her feet. It was the loss of a great part of herself that she was grieving for.

And here came her own daughter, walking into her mothering shade. Alice, leaf-dappled green and gold all over her pale dress, her turbulently unkempt red hair, coming calling her in.

'Mum? Spare a moment?'

'Coming,' said Marian. She felt the wrench – the weight of being mother, and not daughter, like a crack in the heartwood of the world.

Alice came to her, lifted Marian's arm across her bony shoulder, and twined her waist as they walked together back toward the house – meaning, no doubt, only a gentle show of love, but as one helps a casualty to walk.

In the barn the pictures were waiting, sorted. Leo had finished, taken his rucksack, and left.

'Look, Mum,' Alice said. She was pointing to a smallish painting, done on board. The scene was of a golden beach, curving like a lateral new moon round a brilliantly azure and improbable sea. A low grassy promontory stretched across the horizon, pointing towards a lighthouse on a rock. A green drum-shaped buoy topped with a slanting yellow pole floated a little way out. The picture had the meticulous, innocent verisimilitude of a diagram, and clear bleached colour – pale sand, peacock sea.

'These ought to be your long lost beaches, Ma,' said Alice. She was holding another picture, showing this time a vast expanse of sand, crossed with a silver-blue streak of water, as of a river reaching the sea across a beach. Behind it the white smoking towers of a power-station rose on a green shore. Unusually for Stella, the picture had a title: Low Tide, St Ives.

'Yes,' said Marian, softly, 'I think they are.' Shining memory stirred, unfocussed as she looked. With the third picture – a view of a beach from above, fringed with raggedy wild flowers, and in prospect the harbour, the chapel on the hill behind it, the crook-armed quay protecting tilted boats, high and dry, she suddenly felt the frame expand, dissolve. She knew that if she turned a little to the right she would see the lighthouse, far away. She knew that just ahead of her to the left a path would plunge down that zigzagged, and took her to dry, silken, engulfing sands at the back of the beach. She knew that behind her was home – the windows and doors standing wide, and the blind billowing stiffly in the breeze, like a salt-encrusted sail. She could hear the tapping of the little acorn-shaped bead on the dangling drawcord on the blind, as it flew in and out across the sill. The knowledge filled her with joy – she could go on and on – she knew how as you ran out into the expanse of sand it hardened under foot, and cooled until you were running on the smooth firm platform left by the falling tide, and then in the glassy waves, the scalloped lace-edged dancing petti-coats of the sea. And if you turned round from there, and looked up you would see . . . memory faltered and fled.

'What do you think, Ma?' said Toby. He had come in behind her, from the house.

'I think I must go there. At once. Today – well, it's a bit far, isn't it? Tomorrow.'

'No problem,' said Toby. 'I'll take you.'

Alice said, 'I think I'd better get back. They'll be working on the next concert by now – in fact I think – Mum, I'm sorry, but I don't think I can go. Do you mind?'

'I'd always rather have you with me,' said Marian. 'But of course you must get back. You have your own life to live. And you've given me all this time already.'

Later Marian found Leo's incriminating receipt had gone from behind the teapot on the dresser. A fifty-pound note was in its place.

She and Toby arrived in darkness. It took longer than they would have thought possible – longer to drive Alice to her London train, close down the unfamiliar house, check the doors and windows and lights, empty the fridge, leave the key with a neighbour, stop the milk, pack their things and load Toby's car. Longer to drive right down England to the end, and into Cornwall. There was plenty to engage the eye in the cloudy-bright, early summer day. The trees in almost Day-Glo green leaf, acres of wheat, acres of barley swathing the gentle lowlands, and giving way to pasture on the uplands, the regions of chalk and bell-barrows, at the heart of which Stonehenge rose suddenly into view, rising from behind a slight crest beside the road.

Beyond Bodmin they were driving across bleak, rather flat land – what in the north was called a 'moss' – barren, marshy, and luridly lit by a sunlight that had slipped under the cloud cover, and was burning like bright embers in the ash. Then the darkness rolled up from the Atlantic, and they saw only road markings, signs, cat's-eyes.

Somewhere along the way, Marian asked, 'Toby, surely that leave you said you were due for must be running out by now, and you show no sign of being bothered at coming this great long way.'

'Don't you want me, Ma?' he said.

'You know I do. But . . .'

Toby explained about insider dealing, which Marian took a while to grasp. About how only a few people had the knowledge which had done the damage, and he was one of them. He admitted being under suspicion, but avoided owning up to any justification for it. He was ashamed to, with a sharpness that took him aback. He mentioned instead that various people senior to him—

'But son, if you say you know who it was, hadn't you better say?' Marian asked him. 'What about your own prospects? Won't you be under a cloud?'

'I'll have to live it down, then,' he said. 'Don't worry about it, Ma.'

'I can't help it,' said Marian. 'It's what mothers do. I'll do it quietly. I'm worried about Alice too. Something's wrong. Do you know about it, Toby?'

'Don't ask me, Ma,' he said. 'I take after you. I don't get it.'

'It's artistic temperament, you mean. It's music?'

'That too. She's had a bust-up with Max.'

'Well, that might not be such bad news in the long run . . . What was it about, do you know?'

'About missing rehearsals to come up to see Gran. He threatened to boot her out of the quartet. She's been worried sick about it.'

'Well, she's gone back now.' Marian was baffled. She was afraid for both her children, afraid for the sudden lacunae in what had seemed lives set fair, and full of prospect. Well, professional prospect, anyway; to be honest, since Toby had no steady girlfriend, and Alice was playing live-in-chattel to a man old enough to be her father, Marian felt no satisfaction with that aspect of their prospects.

At last the signs on the endless road offered St Ives, and they turned off.

'I expect there's a station car-park,' said Toby. 'We'll try and find that while we get our bearings.' There was. The moment they got out of the car they could hear the sea, chuntering away to itself below the wall. Marian crossed the wet tarmac – it had rained in St Ives – and leaned over. She could just discern, faintly pallid in the velvet night air, the white bolsters of foam crossing the beach below her. The air smelled rinsed and salty. 'Oh!' she said.

They walked out of the station, found at once a flight of steps descending, and went down them; instinctively heading for the water's edge. But they were not at the water's edge, but in a narrow little street with steep front gardens to the houses one side, and shoulder to shoulder cottages on the other. It was lit with staccato pools of lamplight, it glistened with rain, and the sound of the sea came over the rooftops in broken gusts. There were wind-harassed plants in window-boxes, and bed and breakfast signs. In a few yards they had found their billet for the night, and Toby went back to fetch their cases.

They were hungry, but there were places to eat – a modest-looking bistro just on the corner. 'Toby,' said Marian, as they strolled back after the meal, 'thank you for coming. I don't think I'd like to be doing this alone.'

But at first she was alone that first morning, because he slept late and she woke early. She woke to the sound of the sea. The well-known, long forgotten sound of clamorous shouted whispers, sighing and shushing with a rhythm of thrusting and withdrawing like sexual play. From where Marian lay it was loud and quite precise, each soft climax an audible ejaculation half a mile wide. The curtains in her room were not drawn quite together, and a dancing undulant riband crossed the ceiling above her bed in a widening net of reflected light.

She drew back the curtain, and found that the window was right over the sea's edge; she found herself looking past the harbour quay, and out over bright blue water to the lighthouse, both suddenly seen and suddenly remembered, mistily white in a hazy morning distance. There were the headlands, the near one green, the further one lilac. And the sea that began beneath her a modest green like the glass of a white wine bottle, deepening to turquoise in the middle distance, had gathered at the horizon a concentration of bright blue fierce enough fully to deserve the name 'ultramarine'. Marian stood tranced, wondering if she was remembering the paintings seen only yesterday – the paintings of the beaches – or something real teasing her from just beyond the limit of recollection, from some time before the dawn of a continuous Marian. She looked at her watch. There was more than an hour to go before breakfast. She got dressed rapidly and went out.

There was a pearly sky, and the golden beach – Porthminster, she gathered from a sign forbidding dogs in summer – had only one other walker. Marian wandered,

deeply bemused, along the beach. The morning light cast
the heights behind the beach into shadow, but there were
houses there, and a bridge of some kind. On her right the
shining bay, still more or less the view from the window
just now. She walked on the glossy slopes of sand just
relinquished by the falling tide, and her footprints filled
with water as she went, and elided behind her. She waved
at the other walker as they passed each other.

'Did you see the seals?' he asked.

'Seals? No! Where?'

He pointed. There were two black faces bobbing just
beyond the breaking surf, that seemed to be staring at
Marian. They were growling and barking at each other in
a kind of grumbling conversation that made Marian and
the stranger laugh.

'There are dolphins, sometimes,' he said, moving on.
But there couldn't be, could there? Certainly there were
none this morning. She watched the seals till they swam
round the rocks of the point at the end of the beach, and
disappeared. The sands ended in a tumbled rocky cliff,
blue-black with mussel shells, and fringed with slippery
gold-brown kelp. Marian turned to walk back.

Facing this way the town was in view, appearing to be
floating high above the water. There was the crooked
sheltering arm of the quay, with its two lighthouses; the
clustered cottages, all roofscape and windows; the white
hotel perched on the rocks, past which she had come
down to the beach. A little square white beach café stood
at the foot of the cliff on her left.

'I have come too far,' she thought. And then: 'How do
I know? Too far for what?'

But, nevertheless, she began to retrace her steps,
walking up the beach as well as along, to go behind the
café. And as if she had known it there was a path there,

ascending the flowery verdancy of the cliff. It took its time over the steep, bending and bending back, crossing the railway line, offering wild garlic and bluebells shrinking into the grass, and the delicate stars of stitchwort to passing walkers, and reaching eventually the viewpoint – precisely the viewpoint – from which Stella's 'Low Tide' picture had been made. There was a little blue painted garden bench set there and Marian sat down on it. Remembering, dreaming, and experiencing had become fused. She did not know which she was doing. From here she could see the sea above and behind the houses round the harbour, and was looking down at and beyond it all. The vistas had the wildness of landscape and the open, dangerous seas as well as the nested safety and friendliness of human habitation. There was freshness in the air as though all the ancient rocks and immemorial sands, and hundred and two-hundred-year-old roofs and mellow walls, had been newly made, mint struck clean that very morning. With a tackety-tack noise, freighted with nostalgia, a train ran into the station, passing just below where she sat. And if she turned her head a little, there across the bay was the lighthouse, emerging from the mists of the morning sharp and clear, as though it had come nearer, bringing its backdrop of receding headlands with it.

It felt like remembering music. As though someone hummed a bar or two of some great music – a Haydn quartet or something – and one's mind began silently singing the rest, phrase after lovely phrase flowing in one's inner ear perfectly replayed. And, of course, home was behind her. Marian found she knew that. She got up, and looked around, turning her back to the sea. Behind her was a gate in a garden wall – or a gap with gateposts, rather, for the gate itself had gone. A blue gate, she remembered, and in the same moment saw the remaining flakes of blue paint on the iron bolts that had formed the hinge, still jutting from the granite posts. She walked in, and ascended a terraced garden, all steps, to a driveway sweeping round a dignified granite house. Bay windows, a stained glass window lighting the stairs, a grand front door between two stone lions, mounting guard.

Marian rang the doorbell. A woman came quickly to the door, and saying, 'You're early,' let her in.

But the moment she was inside, the dream and the recollection faded together. Marian was standing in the hall of a strange house, looking at a stranger.

'I'm sorry,' she said. 'I'm sorry; I used to live here. It would be very kind if you could just let me see my old bedroom—'

'But you can see everything,' the woman said, and then 'Didn't Hickson send you? Aren't you from the agency?'

'No . . . I . . . Are you selling this house?' Marian asked, struggling to keep a hold on reality in the clouds of dreaming.

'Perhaps,' the woman said. 'We might have to consider that. For the moment we are letting it.'

'I'll take it,' said Marian. 'Right through. What will the rent be for a long let?'

'But you haven't seen it yet,' the woman said. 'Don't you want to see it?'

She must, as a child, have spent hours on beach and in garden, and more hours gazing out of windows. Every outlook was familiar, every room unknown. It was a large house, having generously proportioned rooms, with high ceilings and mullioned bay windows. It had four bedrooms – three on the first floor, and one huge attic that stretched from end to end of the roof space, lined with some sort of fragrant wood panelling. A scuffed and scruffy coconut matting covered the floor of this room.

'The floor-covering's not up to scratch here, I'm afraid,' the owner said – she had been making deprecating remarks all round the house, which was furnished modestly enough with family things showing family wear and tear. Now Marian tore her eyes away from the tops of wind-tilted trees showing through the dormer window, and considered the matting.

'It's a big room,' the owner told her. 'New carpeting would cost a lot.'

'But bare boards would look good up here,' said Marian.

'They would cost as much as carpet, I'm afraid,' the owner said, stooping to lift a corner of the matting, and turning several yards of it back. The floor was covered with paint. Not as in a painted floor – but thickly encrusted with daubs and spills and hardened-off worms of colour from tubes, and footprints in spills trodden all over the place and then covered and recovered with more globs and drips, and blots, in violent multicolour – a kind of chaotic graffiti of repeated accident and neglect.

Marian grimaced. 'That will have been Stella,' she said.

'I beg your pardon?'

'Stella Harnaker. My mother. She was an artist. She must have used this room as a studio.'

'We didn't buy from a Harnaker. It was from a Mrs Godfrey.'

'Stella would have been long ago. Before 1945.'

'Well, none of the owners since has faced up to having it stripped. It's all set rock hard, I understand. And we couldn't face it either, we just covered it over and used the attic for a playroom. That's why the matting is shabby, I'm afraid.'

'It doesn't matter,' said Marian. 'Not the matting, not anything. I would like to rent from you for as long as possible.'

'We have somebody coming at nine,' the owner said, unhappily, looking at her watch. 'From the agents. And you are somebody else altogether.'

'I will give you references,' said Marian. 'And three months' rent down. I'll go back to my room and get my cheque book right away – I came without anything – I was just walking before breakfast—'

'You haven't had breakfast?' said the owner. 'I'll make you some coffee and toast. Come and sit in the kitchen and talk to me. After all, the real people are late, and a bird in the hand—'

'I'll be the bird in the hand,' said Marian.

Later, with everything talked over and agreed, she left, and went almost skipping, so light she felt, down the path bending and re-bending to the back of the beach. An extraordinary lightness of heart propelled her – she felt like a kite that flies only when its string is firmly anchored. At the little café – now taking down its shutters and making ready to offer not only vanilla ice-cream but *moules marinière* and grilled megrim sole – she stooped to shed her sandals, and ran sinking into the soft sand, going back along the beach. And here was Toby coming towards her – coming to look for her, of course, though he pretended not to be, and as soon as she was recognized he adopted a swaggering unconcerned manner, as though he just happened to be walking, accidentally to meet her.

'I've rented a house,' she said. 'I'm staying for a while. You too – for as long as you can – if you like, of course.'

She saw in his eyes a strange expression, one that she suddenly recognized, knew must often have been in her own eyes, looking at Stella – that cautious, oh-God-what-next look of child confronting crazy parent. Laughing she said, 'It's all right, it's all right, it's the right one! I must get my cheque book,' she added, and waving at him she ran along the edge of the waves, which now the tide had turned were larger, and pawed at her, jumping at her skirt, and wetting her to above the knees as she ran. 'Three days!' she called back to him, over her shoulder. 'We can have it in three days!'

On that first day Toby set out to explore, to discover where his mother had landed him. He liked exploring. Especially in this kind of weather – cool, bright and breezy, with a salt tang on the air. He was wandering round a tight little town, almost watertight. Built long ago round two ways of making a living, and both of them bloody dangerous – fish and tin. Toby knew about the tin, and knew it was gone now, from reading commodity reports. Nothing left of it to see, above ground. Fishing had come first and lasted longest, though that too had almost gone now. There were a dozen or so little working boats in the harbour, tilting at their moorings on the sand. Having only a half-tide harbour can't have helped. But the town was made for fishermen; it was built along a sandbar between the outer beach and the harbour, running out along to a green headland, with a little mariner's chapel on top, overlooking the warren of streets and clustered houses. It was picturesque – a whole town built on a warren of pilchard cellars round a harbour. Everyone cheek by jowl, packed into little streets you could shake hands across.

There were an amazing number of these narrow little lanes with pretty cottages, making nooks and corners with each other, climbing steeps and twisting round bends, peering at each other through dormer windows, shuffling shoulder to shoulder, jostling each other for 'Sea Glimpses'. The most cursory glance in the estate agents' windows – Toby liked to keep an eye on property prices – revealed how desirable 'Sea Glimpses' were; those, and parking places. The folk who built the town had not been interested in either. Well, Toby thought, of course they weren't interested in parking, though they might have been interested in bringing a cart to the door, and some of these narrow ginnels, these stepped alleyways, and enclosed courtyards, would not have allowed even that. And how odd it seemed that they positively turned their backs to the sea, and unfortunate really, now that they earned a living from doing bed and breakfast for tourists. But even in an irregular little square, or a crooked street in which the sound of the sea rocked to and fro and caressed his hearing, no prospect of the sea itself was possible. As though once they were home and dry, he reflected, they didn't want to know, they didn't want to see. And perhaps they didn't, perhaps that was right.

Although, how could they not? he wondered, seeing down a steeply descending street a stretch of harbour water, not blue at all, but blazing golden-green, and sparkling with sprinkled stars of incandescent and extinguished highlights. He went down towards it at once.

And then there were boats. Very little boats in most of the harbour, but maybe a dozen fishing boats, using the quay. And one superb yacht, anchored a little way out. Toby looked at it lustfully, assessing its clean lines, guessing at the cost. He loved boats. His father in America had taught him sailing. He had a sailing boat in San Francisco Bay. Nothing in Toby's life so far had given him more joy than the lean of a boat in the wind, the start-up of the babbling water under the prow. Now he stood on the end of the quay looking at the yacht, musing for quite a time.

While he was standing there a little fishing boat came bustling in, with a trail of shrieking gulls behind it, like dragged, tattered bunting. He smiled as it reminded him of a plough pursued across the fields – 'I will sail the briny ocean, I will plough the salt sea . . .' he hummed to himself.

Someone yelled, 'Hey, Mathy!' and a serpentine rope came sailing up from the boat deck twenty feet below him. He caught it easily, one-handed, and swiftly twisting loop on loop dropped a clove hitch over the nearest bollard, and drew it tight. 'Come for a drink?' said the voice below. ''Ang on and come for a drink?'

But the favour didn't seem worth the payment, and, embarrassed, suddenly shy, Toby walked away. Away from the harbour, into the warren of streets, and out again, finding himself looking up across the grassy hill to the chapel. Once up there he could see yet another prospect of the town.

Toby sat down on a wooden bench in the lee of the chapel wall, out of the wind, to look at the spectacular vistas of golden beaches, both sides of the headland, and the Victorian town, a result of the railway, clearly, clambering back up the inland slopes. An old man was already sitting there, his hands crossed on his walking-stick, a fat little dog lying on the ground at his feet.

'Handsome day,' he said to Toby.

'Glorious,' said Toby. 'Wonderful light. Is it always like this?'

'Bless you, boy, not always. Different every day. That's why the artists come.'

'I don't always expect to see what the artists say they see,' said Toby. 'But I can see this . . .'

'It's quite real,' the man said. 'We be upwind of everything in England that makes dust. Including all the ploughing. It's dangerous light – you wouldn't believe how quick the tourists skinburn. You won't catch local people 'alf naked on the beaches.'

'Are you local?' asked Toby.

'No. I'm not local, I'm a native,' the man said. When Toby blinked he explained, 'Locals live here. Natives were born here.'

'I suppose if you're a native, tourists are hard to bear,' said Toby.

'They're a living,' the man said. 'And it's not as bad as it used to be. The rabble go to the Costa Brava now. We do prefer the artists; they're more faithful, year-round.'

'Who am I speaking to?' asked Toby. The dog was pulling on the leash now, and his companion got up to go.

'I'm Mr Stevens,' the man said. 'But so's half the rest of the town. If you wanted to find me you'd have to ask for Nubby. Nubby Stevens.'

'Nubby?' said Toby.

'There's not enough names to go round,' Mr Stevens said. 'Not enough surnames and not enough Bible names to tell us apart. There might be twenty Matthew Stevens in the town. But everyone knows who Bish and Bar and Dinks and Nubby are.'

He took his dog off on the rest of its walk, and Toby sat on for a while.

Then he walked round the headland, upon whose rocks the sea was energetically leaping, until the outer beach came into view, spectacular with booming surf a mile long and a mile deep. Even in the chill of the smart offshore wind the beach had children playing. And the surf was peppered with surfers, floating like huge black sea birds, or rising suddenly atop a crest to ride to a fall in the wave-breaks. Toby watched, resolving to try that. His gaze took in the shore, the rocky point beyond the beach, the sloping churchyard, crowded with men at anchor – the embattled run of old buildings – workshops? Sail lofts? And the snazzy modern flats which lined the back of the beach. As he watched, the yacht from the bay came suddenly into view, scudding across the skyline, in full sail, leaning to the wind, and making speed. Where could she be going? Toby wondered. What was out there? Cork? Fastnet? Newfoundland? The Scillies? Or round Land's End? With all his heart he longed to be aboard her, cutting free, outbound, setting a course.

Marian was walking too. She was lost, and also disorientated. The town she walked in flickered in and out of memory, alternating places she could recall with uncanny accuracy, down to the shape of the shadow cast across the street, the skew of the lines of cobbles, with places she had never been in before in her life, the commonplace generic seaside town, unknown to her. And then round another corner she would be standing in the light of childhood, looking at the lighthouse framed in a gap between houses, back in a world where everything was perfectly placed. The street names – or passage names, rather – amused and confused her. Nothing could be much less square than Island Square – was Teetotal Street then a hive of drunkenness? And what about Virgin Street? No doubt the virtues of the original inhabitants were better than their geometry. She tried to make mental notes of the whereabouts of useful shops – a hardware store, a greengrocer, a real fishmonger, an old fashioned draper, a newsagent, among the plethora of shops packed with tourist tat.

Among those, she liked the one selling shells. But for the most part they were horrific. Sixties style kitsch beads and droopy shirts printed with suns and moons; tortured glass and brass, model creatures and luridly furry stuffed toys; mountains and mountains of fudge in yucky flavours . . . She smiled to herself, and promised herself a competition with Toby, to find the nastiest thing on sale in the town. And paintings. What was different from other seaside resorts was the number of 'galleries' selling paintings. Obviously the visitor to St Ives was expected to think that a painting would be a good souvenir. For the most part the paintings she passed by were *dire* – unbelievably bad. Unpaintings. They wouldn't clean your eyeballs, and sharpen up your view of the world, they would clutter them, with a double whammy of awfulness. First with a sort of stupid prettification, an intent to show even this spectacular place in the light of any old beauty spot, and then with technical incompetence, so that the intended selective realism was botched and only half achieved. There were far too many sails and sunsets for probability.

There was also an inescapable impression of haste, as though the artist had not had time to look carefully before slapping on the paint. However terrible some of the 'souvenirs', it would surely be one of these daubed canvases or boards that would win the prize nomination for the nastiest thing on sale in St Ives. Compared to the best of these, *anything* by Stella was a masterpiece! Marian shuddered. These things overwhelmed her with an unpleasant feeling of pity and contempt. Pity and contempt for the artists who had perpetrated them.

At twelve Toby bought a beer in the Sloop at the harbour-side, and carried it outside to drink it in the sun, view-gazing. A lot of other people had the same idea, and he was standing in a basking and chattering crowd. Was there another pub by the lifeboat shed? he wondered, for there too was a cluster of people, leaning on the railings. As he watched the glass doors of the boat-shed opened, up-and-over style – it was a snazzy crisp new building – and the boat nosed out, and lurched forward to stand poised at the top of the ramp. Then, with an almost sinister deliberate purpose, like something advancing on an assailant, it came on down the ramp. Near the bottom someone in yellow oilskins ducked under the looming prow to unhitch it from the trolley. Toby stared at it, seeing in everything about it, seeing in its fitness for its purposes, the illimitable, motiveless destructive strength of the sea. In its deep blue sculpted hull with the white Plimsoll line below and the scarlet stripe at the gunwale, drawing its shape to his attention; in the orange superstructure, ready to be battened down, he saw the strength and swell of storm waves; in the battery of radar equipment she carried he saw the immensity of the ocean, in which every ship was lonely, potentially lost, without these slender links, 'all at sea'.

The boat, suddenly precipitate, dashed into the water at the foot of the ramp, and roared round a wide turning circle in the brimming harbour, making out to sea beyond the quay. A wide and foaming wake remembered her course behind her, fading and spreading slowly in the aftermath. Where was she going? he wondered, finishing his beer – who was in trouble? Not some child on an inflatable mattress this time – they had an inshore lifeboat for that sort of thing. With a leap of his heart he thought of the lovely yacht he had seen just a while ago. Could it be her? He minded that thought hideously, and though of course he could see with part of his mind that danger to life on a battered and ugly coaster or tanker was morally speaking just as serious, the beauty of the sailing boat, and the idea of free force, speeding on the wind, that she represented made him care nothing at that moment for morality.

He returned his glass, and positively ran along the wharf, dodging the strollers, past the amusement arcades with their shoddy and flashy temptations and blaring sounds, and reached the dispersing crowd at the top of the launching ramp.

'What was it?' he asked, directing his question to two vaguely official-looking men who were standing talking by the doors of the looming empty boat shed. 'What did they go out to?'

They seemed surprised, and did not answer him at once.

'Was it that yacht that was anchored here last night?' he asked.

'Bless you, it idn't for real,' one of them said. 'Only practice. When it be real you'll hear the rockets go up for the crew to muster.'

'Thanks,' said Toby, feeling slightly foolish. But the man nodded to him, friendly enough, and said, 'I know you, don't I?'

'I don't think so,' said Toby. 'It's my first time here.'

'My mistake then. Thought I'd a seen you somewhere afore.' He turned back to his companion, and Toby, hands in pockets, wandered off.

Marian was buying things. She had agreed with Mrs Veal that the house should be rented furnished; but the agreement excluded bedding and towels, china and cutlery, and some of the kitchen equipment – Marian had agreed immediately that Mrs Veal was to take with her anything she needed to help her set up home with her daughter. Marian would simply buy replacements. She had been offered a reduction in the proposed rent to take account of the required expense. And now she stood in White's in Fore Street, choosing things.

She had an agreeable sense of wild luxury and self-indulgence, piling on the counter top sheets and bottom sheets and pillow cases in matching sets, piles of pink towels, piles of white towels, piles of blue towels. A green and white gingham tablecloth caught her eye, and she bought that too. And then coarse linen bedspreads, creamy white with a pattern in the weave . . . she had never done anything like this before. When she and Donald set up house money was in short supply, and she had started with wedding presents, chosen, however lovingly, by other people. And then one replaced things piecemeal, as this and that wore out. Soon nothing matched, nothing was a complete set, and thrift and familiarity worked together to keep things like that.

Now suddenly, she was buying things all together. From White's, who would deliver her purchases the next day, she proceeded to Woolworths, where stainless steel kitchen thingummies seemed cheap and serviceable, and she envisioned a whole kitchen equipped in steel and clear glass, not a countrified patterned pot anywhere, and began to put that too into effect. She had set herself a problem carrying things, but luckily she no sooner emerged from Woolworths' lower floors onto the wharf than she bumped into Toby, and despatched him to get the car. She was childishly happy. How wonderful to choose everything without compromising with Donald's tastes, or, even worse, his mother's – all white damask and patterned silver plate. And how relatively affordable it had been to be rich for a morning! She was avoiding thinking forward; she had not considered what she would do with all the lovely new things when the lease ended, when she had to go home. No, when she had to go away from home. Surrounded by carrier bags and parcels she sat on a seat by the harbour, listening to lapping water, and watching the reticulate reflections wavering on the side of a pretty moored boat. People wandered past her, and snatches of their talk mixed with the raucous calls of the ubiquitous gulls. How could any creature look so graceful, and sound so vulgar?

Toby wasn't long. They drove the clobber up to the house, and discovered that Mrs Veal was leaving early – they could be in by tomorrow if they liked. Before they went out to dinner that night Toby rang Alice and put the address of the house on her answerphone.

'How does it strike you, Toby?' Marian asked him that evening. 'St Ives, I mean. I can hardly tell. I can't see it as if for the first time; it keeps doing vivid flashbacks at me.'

'It's lovely,' he said. 'A lovely empty shell. Well, not completely empty—'

'Whatever do you mean?'

'It was shaped for a way of life. For fishing, for people who lived cheek by jowl and worked together closely. Like a shell that's shaped round a living creature, and left empty when it dies.'

'And the tourists bustle round in it, like hermit crabs in a shell?' she said, amused.

'Yes. First artists, then tourists.'

'I expect part of what one likes is the sense of that tight-knit life,' Marian said. 'The shape of it. People don't live like that any more, knowing all the neighbours. We're all more or less alone. It must have been very close and kindly.'

'And bitchy too, I expect,' said Toby.

The house had a big bay window to the living room. Its tall mullions divided the view into three; from the left-hand pane a dazzling prospect of beach below, then the sweep of the town round the harbour, the arm of the quay extending forward, embracing the boats. From the right-hand pane one looked across the bay to the lighthouse on its dark pyramid of rock, and given clear light further headlands fading with distance, one beyond another.

Through the middle pane a mysterious prospect of pure sea, a simple line dividing air and water, each changing in an endless panorama of ephemeral effect. It was mesmerizing. Once they were in the house they spent hours simply gazing out. 'Look at it now,' they said to each other – and in a minute's space, 'Look at it *now*!'

'Why do I like lighthouses so much?' Marian wondered aloud.

'Phallic symbols?' said Toby, suppressing a grin.

'Oh, rubbish, son,' said Marian.

Toby came to stand behind her in the window, looking out. The view had changed again; an inky and blurred cloud on the skyline was casting rainbows. 'Monuments to altruism, more like.'

'What do you mean?' asked Marian. She could not bear to turn round to ask the question.

'It's in everyone's interest to have them, but in no-one's to provide them,' said Toby. 'We like them because they show us that people sometimes act unselfishly. Sometimes.'

He sounded a little wistful. But Marian, who would have liked to question him, thought better of it.

They had been settled in the house for a week when Alice reappeared. Toby let her in, and she marched into the centre of the living room, put down her bag and her viola case, and said:

'I've come.'

'Darling, how lovely—' Marian looked up from writing letters.

'I take it there's room for me?'

'Of course there is. There's even a nice new quilt on the bed. Bring your things and I'll show you.'

'No rehearsals, sib?' said Toby from the foot of the stairs, as they ascended.

'No!' said Alice, in almost a shout. 'I wouldn't be here, otherwise, stupid!'

'Sorry I spoke,' said Toby.

Later Alice sat morosely, silently, staring at the view. 'Do you remember this, Mum?' she asked.

'Half and half. It's a funny sensation.'

'Oh – I met Leo on the train.'

'Leo? Coming here?'

'Yes; he lives here. He said he had a place in London, but he lives here. He said as soon as the train got round the headland he could feel it drawing him back.'

'Well what was he doing in Cambridge, then?' asked Toby.

'Visiting Gran, I suppose. Coming to her funeral. Helping with pictures.'

Wanting money, added Marian to herself. She braced herself for Leo to reappear.

There was an oddity, of course, in settling in to live together, even only for a while, mother and grown children making up a family again. They had partly forgotten each other, or perhaps they had cheated memory by changing. Did Toby always sing so loudly, and take baths at such curious times? Didn't he once like peanut butter, which he now refuses? Did he and Alice always talk so incessantly, arguing and quarrelling about every possible thing? Perhaps they did. Alice had always washed her hair every day, and left clothes lying around on all the chairs. Alice had always practised for several hours a day – had it always sounded so urgent, so raw? Perhaps it had. While it lasted it filled the house with a feeling of struggle and loss. Perhaps, Marian thought, it was just that Alice had once played more cheerful music, or much easier music. Toby seemed unable to live without watching video movies, and had rented a set with a video recorder. Night after night as Marian was going to bed they settled into the armchairs to watch something borrowed from the video shop, that would run till well after midnight. Toby poured them a malt whisky apiece. They bought the drink themselves these days; they offered to pay for their phone calls.

And something really had changed greatly, from Marian's point of view; she had become what she never was in their childhood and adolescence, an object of their attention. Marian herself, her moods, needs, quirks, faults, virtues, had become a presence in the group. She had lost the quality of parent that made her once a kind of permanently non-playing captain of the team. Or perhaps it was the role of referee that she had lost; certainly they no longer appealed to her for justice, or even for sympathy, but fought each other without recourse. Of course it was because of her that they were down here, playing house. But it was more than that. If they call her 'the AP' – 'Aged Parent', Alice explained – if they humoured her, it was as they might humour each other. 'Did Stella and I ever reach this stage?' Marian wondered. 'No, we did not,' she answered herself. 'I was never as old a daughter as Alice has become.'

Also, since she remembered them as a good deal of

unremitting hard work, Marian was surprised at the effect of three pairs of hands on the chores of living. There was willing help, instantly, almost unthinkingly given. They washed their own clothes, they did the shopping, they even washed up after supper, and took turns at cooking. It was easier than living alone! And there was time, therefore, to stare at the sea, the sky, the lighthouse, and murmur, 'Look at it now . . .'

'I'd like to go there,' Marian said, softly.

'Where?' asked Alice.

'To the lighthouse. To land there.'

'Oh, I asked about that, the other day,' said Toby, looking up from his book. 'No such trip. They gave me two reasons. No demand, and dangerous water. Look,' – he came to stand beside her at the window – 'see all that broken water running out along the horizon? That's a half-tide reef; that's what the lighthouse warns of. So it probably is dangerous.'

'I expect altruism usually is,' said Marian. And now, to the delectable remoteness of the white tower on the black surf-girdled rock, was added the strong pull of inaccessibility, impossibility. Yet from everywhere you went in the town the lighthouse could be seen.

The day came when Marian came back from shopping in the town to find a familiar duffel bag on the doorstep. Leo was sitting in the porch.

'You found it, then?' he said.

'What?'

'Stella's. First place I looked for you.'

'It's mine now,' said Marian. 'For a while,' she added, deferring to truth. 'I gather you live here, Leo? I somehow supposed you lived in Cambridge.'

'I work all over the place,' he said. 'But I live in St Ives.'

'Well,' she said, putting down her shopping, and opening the inner door to the house, 'cup of tea? Stay to supper? The young will be home by and by.'

'Remember all this then, do you?' he said, following her in. 'Lumme – it's gone a bit different though. Never used to be clean or tidy, in the good old days!'

'Try looking under the carpet in the attic room,' said Marian.

'Jesus, is that Jackson Pollock floor still there?' he said. 'We should try cutting it into squares and selling it to the Tate!'

They were smiling at each other, like old friends. Like people with shared memories, waiting for the kettle to boil.

'Leo . . .'

'Yes?'

'You put on quite a performance when we first met. You were so truly awful – do you always try to make people dislike you?'

'Yes,' he said, 'I suppose so.'

'Why?'

'In case they do.'

'I don't think I quite get that.'

'Well, if people dislike me,' he said, 'at least I know why. You've changed your mind about me; but if you hadn't—'

'You would have been able to blame me.'

'Exactly.'

'Leo – that money . . .'

'I will need it sometime. But I've raised it for now.'

She couldn't help, evidently, her surprise showing on her face.

'You thought I hadn't two beans? Well, at a pinch I have one bean. I've pawned my house. Remortgaged it.'

'My God, Leo – what if her estate isn't enough – what if—'

He shrugged. 'More fool me in that case.'

Alice had driven Toby from the house. The endless grinding music from her room, the edgy, restless company she made, oppressed him. It was a squally day, in which the rain lashed the window-panes, and the lighthouse retreated into invisibility in the occluded air. Marian was tidying and cleaning the house – both of them prowling around him. He suddenly found the company of women overpowering, and at a break in the rain he bolted from the house, and plunged down the hill into the town. There he took shelter from another squall in a sports shop, and spent some time trying walking boots. Then he bought boots, a good waterproof windcheater, and a map of the coast path, and set off.

Beyond the town the land turned rugged. Great outcrops of rocks broke the skylines, and green fields sloped to the brink of precipitous cliffs. The path snaked along the top of the cliffs, margined in wild flowers, and giving astonishing, thunderous prospects of roaring coves. Great vistas of grey-blue sea spread away to his right, to a smudged horizon, a blotted out margin between grey water and grey sky. The wind tugged and buffeted him, and his spirits lifted as he walked. Gradually the clouds were being torn apart by the wind, and giving rags of blue sky, and sudden fragments of sunshine edged with rainbow.

Toby walked almost at a run, going as fast as the roughness of the path permitted, pushing himself. He drew great lungfuls of the dust-free air. Miles out from the town he stood in the lee of a great cairn of huge fractured boulders that seemed to totter on the brink, but had probably been standing for a thousand years unchanged. It was surprisingly warm in its shelter. He felt exultant, clean. Everything round him was worn down to basics. He remembered London with panic and distaste, thrust the thought away, and walked on.

He turned back at last, thinking that he ought not to risk blisters from new boots, though they felt OK. He still had his shoes of course, one in each pocket. The squalls had gone rushing up channel, leaving a shining calm in their wake. As he came back within view of the town the graveyard caught his eye, the landed flock of gull-coloured stones and crosses, settled on the green slope above the outer beach, and he mounted the steps to go that way, and lingered in the rosy light of early evening. It gave him a pleasing sort of melancholy to read the headstones. 'An unknown seaman, washed up, drowned.' Names recurred, the names of the bedrock people – Paynter and Stevens and Barber and Care and Cocking. Toby wandered, hands in pockets, along the rows. In the middle of the graveyard a little pair of chapels, joined like Siamese twins, presided. If he looked east the back of the Island, grass and rocks and its own little chapel, rose at an angle, closing the beach, but giving, over its shoulder, a different prospect to the lighthouse. Below the wall the ocean shuttled up and down the beach, sighing softly.

A good place to come to rest, Toby thought, though

perhaps all these seafarers, those drowned and those surviving for their natural term, no more wanted eternity in sight and sound of the tides than they had wanted 'Sea Views' from their cottages? Moments later he found 'Matthew Barber, Lost in the lifeboat disaster, 1939.'

That must be the story that Leo told us, he thought, and, quieted for the moment, headed up to the road.

At the crest of the hill the town crowded up to the top graveyard wall, and then plunged down towards the church. 'Barnoon' Toby read on a road sign. He started down it, lost in thought. Below him the top of the church tower rose up towards his level. Gulls screamed overhead, music thrummed from an open window, and somebody was yelling for someone called Mathy. The sounds made discords around him. 'Mathy, *Mathy*!' Clattering footsteps behind him. 'Be 'ee deaf, Mathy, for Lord sakes . . .'

Toby was trotting down the steps beside the steeply sloping road, when a hand fell on his shoulder. 'Mathy . . .'

He looked round, confronting a young man of his own age and height, who at once withdrew the commanding hand, and said, 'Oh, aa, sorry. Took you for someone else.'

The degree of surprise on the stranger's face amounted to consternation. He disappeared rapidly, dashing off down the rest of the slope and turning left down a side-alley. Leaving Toby mystified enough to tell Alice about it, later.

Going to bed so late, always outlasting their mother's stamina, gave Toby and Alice time to talk together, which they needed to do, knowing things about each other which Marian did not. You could hardly find two more different people out of the same nest, she would have said. And she was right in a way. But difference did not impede perception.

'You must look very like this Mathy,' Alice said, when Toby told his tale. 'Was it a local voice? Was he a St Ives man?'

'Yes.'

'So Mathy is probably local too. Do you think grand-father was local and you look like him, whoever he was?'

'Well, *perhaps*,' said Toby doubtfully.

Slouched in an easy chair while the video tape of *The Age of Innocence* tickered back to the beginning, and the rewind light blipped on the machine, he observed, trying not to, but unable to block it out, that Alice, sitting bare-foot, her blazing red hair untied and drifting across her shoulders, had an expression of desolation.

'What's up, sib?' he asked, lifting a narrow strand of her straying hair, and winding it gently round his finger. 'Are you worried about the Aged Parent wild-goose chasing after the missing ancestor?'

'That too,' she said.

'So what first?'

'Well, you for one thing. Might you go to prison?'

'Ah. No. I might lose my job.'

'But you did do it – this funny dealing thing?'

'Sort of. It's a very grey area, that's the trouble. And I was one of several.'

'I hate to think of you not being honest, Toby.'

'So do I,' he said. 'So do I. But I just lost my foothold, somehow.'

'What will happen to you?'

'Nothing much. They are looking for someone to carry the can for everyone else. So that they can say, "We found the rotten apple, and got rid of it." And I don't know who they'll pick on. It might well be me. Will you cast me out of your life?'

'Can't, can I?' she said. 'You just *are* my brother, stupid.'

'Thanks,' he said. But he could not fool himself that the bleakness in her had anything to do with him. 'What else?' he asked her, gently unwinding her strand of hair, which he had been wearing like a ring.

'Max,' she said. 'I've quarrelled with Max.'

'And there really aren't any rehearsals?'

'He said not. He'll let me know.'

'Don't call him, he'll call you? He's such a *shit*, sib,' said Toby.

'What difference does that make?' she said.

'Well, some. Doesn't it?'

'No, not really. Love is a bit like talent, it just strikes where it strikes. It isn't connected to anything else, either one way or the other.'

'I don't understand,' he said.

'I know you don't,' she said. 'I don't hold it against you. And you will, when it happens to you.'

Marian could see the visitor coming, though she did not at first, of course, realize that the woman was coming to her. Marian was looking through the garden gate, a trowel in her hand, with which she had been planting nerines, a whimsical act, she knew, for a tenant gardener. She stood in the gate, half the lumpy bulbs planted, half still in the bag, and looked at the path, now tarmacadamed, but then, surely, a rough track. A pearly light from a bright cloudy sky cast a porcelain glaze over the evening scene. Her feet remembered the precipitate descent to the beach, but she stood still, and watched the woman on two sticks struggle up the slope towards her. If she was going to run down onto the sands she should wait till the poor creature was safely past her; probably though, she was simply going to turn away, and plant the other nerines.

When she finished, and went in, she found the visitor sitting in the porch, outside the open front door. Having passed the back gate she had gone round to the front of the house, and was waiting.

'I heard there were Harnakers here again,' she said. 'I saw from the papers that Stella is dead. I'm so sorry . . . You are Marian, then.'

'Marian Easton. Yes. Stella Harnaker was my mother. You are some friend of hers?'

'Oh, yes. I am Violet. Violet Garthen.'

At Marian's blank expression she said, 'Unknown to you, I see. Unheard of, my usual fate. But I once knew your mother well. You too, in fact.'

'Come in,' said Marian. 'I'll pour you a sherry. Tell me about it.'

But the visitor seemed to have little urge to narrate. She looked blankly round the living room, and lowered herself gradually into a chair, leaning her sticks against the arm. 'You don't take after her then, I see,' she said.

'What do you mean, Mrs – Miss? Garthen.'

'Miss. Call me Violet. You keep things tidy. You should have seen it when I lived here.'

'You lived here?'

'You don't remember? Well, perhaps you wouldn't. I shared with Stella for a summer, until we quarrelled. It was bloody chaotic. And you were not tidy in those days.'

'I really don't remember, I'm afraid. Are you an artist?'

'Yes, I am. I make – made – prints. Stella didn't think much of them.'

'So she gave you a hard time?' Marian suppressed the ghost of a smile.

'I escaped. I admired her very much at the time.'

'But you tried to share a house with her? Was that wise?'

'There was a war on. Nobody had any money. Sharing was better than starving.'

'Of course. I think you might be the only person left who remembers me as a child. How curious.'

'I don't know much about children. You were something of a nuisance, but perhaps not more than most.'

'I was a nuisance? Playing with your gravers and spilling the etching acid?'

'That sort of thing. Inclined to wander off.'

And Marian winced, hearing in that accusation the diverted attention of the grown-ups, all of them, both of them, preoccupied with other things, so that she was perpetually seen as an interruption. Had she really been a trouble to this stranger?

'I'm sorry,' she said. 'Let me take you to dinner some time next week, and you can tell me all about it.' For she had bought three plump mackerel for supper and could see no way to make three fishes do for four. 'And shall I run you home?' She hoped that dislike did not ring audibly in her voice. It was so clear to her and so groundless.

'I both look and feel like a crab on these sticks,' said Violet. 'But I am supposed to walk. So, no, thank you. But what I came for was to ask you what you propose to do with Stella's pictures. Are they for sale?'

'Some of them will be. I take it you would like one?'

'Very much, if I can afford it.'

'Oh, it won't have to depend on that. If you can remember a particular one and describe it to me, I'll try to find it for you.'

'You are very kind, Stella's daughter,' said Violet dryly, heaving herself to her feet, and leaning on her sticks again. 'And where do you get that from?'

Seeing her to the gate, for the garden was steeply terraced and surely not safe for her, Marian thought to say, 'Did you – do you – know a man called Leo Vincey?'

'I know him,' said Violet. 'He's a fake.'

'*He's* a fake? What do you mean?'

'That awful war,' said Violet, suddenly vehement, 'all the flotsam and jetsam of Europe landed up here. Frightened to stay in London. Too wimpy to fight. Putting their wretched botches and daubs up to the exhibition hanging committees, curling their lips at real artists with a lifetime's devotion behind their skills. Founding break-away societies, quarrelling, making trouble. The place never recovered, to my mind. We all suffered from it.'

'But what has this to do with Leo?' asked Marian.

'Well, among the other things the modernists visited on us was a vogue for local talent,' Violet said. 'They went and "discovered" a poor old sod of a rag-and-bone man, and puffed him as some kind of untaught genius. Working on broken fish-crates and cardboard boxes, about like a three-year-old. Ludicrous. Next thing you know the town is full of artists; fishermen, grocers, window-cleaners, everyone can do it. You can sell a vile ignorant daub for more than a serious etching. That Leo . . . He's plain Leonard, really, of course. Just a skiff boy.'

'What did Stella think about all this?' asked Marian. She really would take Violet out to dinner and pump her exhaustively, but still couldn't resist asking, this minute, at the open door.

'She even went down and bought some of Wallis's stuff,' said Violet. 'She let it get to her, God forgive her.'

'Is that what you quarrelled about?' Marian asked.

'Oh, no,' said Violet, giving Marian a curious sideways stare. The deep wrinkles of age had bitten in a fixed expression on her face that was stronger than any passing expressive one, and made her hard to read, like a page already scrawled over. 'Do you really not remember? We quarrelled about you. I'm off, but I'll hold you to that offer.'

God might forgive Stella, but Violet won't, thought Marian to her departing back. What a termagant! No worse than Stella herself, I suppose. And I wonder if her work is any good – I must try to see some. As if I could tell – how does one tell? And they quarrelled about me?

Toby had become sensitive to the sound of footfalls behind him – to any sense of pursuit. Someone running behind him along Fore Street and shouting 'Oi!' led him, therefore, without looking round, to turn abruptly to the left, up a side street. He turned and stood waiting, expecting to see the runner, whoever it was, hurtle past across the bottom of the alley. But instead the pursuers – there were two of them – swung round the corner after him, and came abruptly face to face with him. They were both youths, younger than Toby, certainly, but one of them was six foot tall and heavy. He had a shaven head, blue with faint stubble, tattoos on both forearms, and an earring. They were standing staring at him, lolling against each other. There was a sort of speculative determination on their faces which convinced him they were hunting him. The shorter one had a shuttle loaded with blue cord in his right hand. Toby walked straight towards them, and past them, back into the narrow little main street, and the crowds of shoppers, without looking back.

He dodged into Rose Lane, and Norway Lane, through St Peter's Street and Fish Street into Island Square. There he stopped, listened, and looked round. The same two rounded the corner just behind him. They came with unmistakable deliberation, a challenging swagger. There couldn't be any doubt about it, really; they *must* be following him.

In which case they could damn well have a run for their money. Abruptly Toby took to his heels, speeding away down Back Road East as fast as he could leg it. When he had shaken them off he slowed down, smiling grimly to himself. Then suddenly he was face to face with the pursuers again, only now there were four of them – one a girl. They were waiting for him at the top of the hill. He turned round and found his way back blocked – three youths with linked arms were standing across the road behind him. But in this town there was always an alley, or a flight of narrow steps. He bolted down the nearest one. It was a courtyard, dark and cramped and full of dustbins, and he thought he was cornered for a moment, but there was in fact a little passageway leading through to another street. He shot out of this like a cork from a bottle, turned and swerved towards the harbour, where there would be people flocking. He preferred a crowd of people. A game like this – surely it was a game? – could turn nasty. What did they want? Why hadn't he asked them, instead of playing catch? But once you ran there was a hunt, and you were the quarry. Toby was nearly afraid, and still running.

Of course he couldn't escape them in this warren of streets, which they knew backwards, and he not at all. He bolted down Bethesda Hill, and they came racing out of a parallel street – six of them now. They linked arms, and came towards him. He spun on his heel, and dived back into Bethesda Hill, leaping up its steep steps. Then he made the inevitable mistake. He chose Carnglaze, and they were close behind him. Turning right at the end of Carnglaze he found them doggedly advancing along the back of the harbour, and his only way to go turned out to be out along Smeaton's Quay – a stony cul-de-sac standing out into water and sand. He might even have jumped and swum for it if the tide hadn't been rather low. So he turned at bay, breathing heavily.

There were more of them than before – a pack of nine or so. They were all looking hard at him, with confrontational curiosity.

'What do you want?' he said. He was angry. If they wanted his money they'd have to fight him for it. In the back of his mind he tried to measure the drop to the sand behind him, the probable damage from being thrown over. 'What the hell are you chasing me for?'

'Chasing?' one of them said. 'Wudn' be chasing if you wadn' running. Why run? Just because we want you t'come for a drink.'

'I'm not going anywhere with you!' said Toby.

'And if we say you are?' the tall one said. Whereupon the girl pushed her way to the front, said, 'Hang on; don't hassle him,' and looking at Toby said, 'Come on, my cock. What harm can you come to having a drink in the Sloop?' She even offered a half-hearted placatory smile.

Toby shrugged, and his captors surrounded him and marched him off the quay and along the wharf. He supposed it was true they could hardly be intending to set upon him in broad daylight, or mug him in the Sloop, but he could feel their tension, them nerving themselves for something. When they reached the dark little door of the inn one of them lifted the latch of the door to the bar, and someone pushed him between the shoulder blades, and propelled him through.

After the bright day outside the bar was dark. Toby blinked. He appeared to be there already, sitting at one of the long tables with a glass of beer in front of him. It was like looking in a mirror in a nightmare – one of those horrible transformation nightmares, in which you dream yourself displaced, in the wrong life – facing him was his twin, nearly. Looking very like him, though more tanned. His hair was cut very short – the skin of his skull glinted through it. Like his friends he was wearing tattoos and earrings. This fellow looked long and levelly at Toby. Then, 'I'm Matthew Huer,' he said. 'And who do you be?'

Marian was happily prowling, a brief shopping list in her handbag, riding the lift to her spirits that ambient beauty gave to plain days. The light danced on the water in the harbour, and the colours of everything seemed peculiarly unmixed – the green of the grassy sloping Island intensely green, the sea an amazing blue, the sand pure chrome, as though the town and its setting had been painted out of a little box of primary colours. She crossed the road to lean over the wall and look down at the beach, the rioting waters of the sea. And felt it somehow, in her arm and fingers – thought of scribbling the surf in white chalk on the sort of blue sugar paper she had been given to scrawl on at nursery school, felt the ghostly movement that would drive the spiralling thick lines – the steady lateral pull to draw the line of silver on the horizon – was there silver chalk? What colour would she need to make the faded lilac sheen of the draining waters on the wet slopes of the sand, converging, repeatedly confluent like the branches of trees in reverse? Surely she would need oils? Or were there pastels bright enough, in the box Stella had given to Leo, all those years ago?

Nothing could possibly be bright enough, she thought, walking on. She passed an art shop and paused to gaze through the window. A collection of posters pinned up at the edge of the window advertised various events. Someone would demonstrate print-making at The St Ives School of Artists, where, also, you could take a life class for four pounds, open to all, beginners welcome. There was an exhibition of work at sale prices by Violet Garthen, in the artist's own home, at the address below.

Violet Garthen lived in a part of the town Marian had never visited before, well inland, with no outlook to the sea. She showed Marian into her front room. It was the bay-windowed best room of a tight little Victorian terrace house, furnished stylishly in an outdated style – a cane-and-cushions settee, a glass-topped table with art books, an overflowing bookshelf built into an alcove, an upright piano on one wall.

'Could I see some of your work?' Marian asked.

'Up there,' said Violet. 'Excuse me if I stay put. I don't like watching people look.'

Marian walked upstairs. The front upstairs room, the largest in the house, was hung round with Violet's work. A chart chest stood against the end wall. Marian looked at the work on the walls, and opened the chart chest to see more. Violet made engravings and lithographs. The engravings were amazing – technically very fine, meticulously detailed and accurate. They showed street scenes with people in curiously old-fashioned clothes. Or flowers. A good one showed a hare in the grass – every blade cut separately. The lithographs were washy in soft colours; sea scenes; several views of moored boats. One could imagine such things looking pleasant and restful on domestic walls. They recorded what one saw; what one already knew that one saw. They demonstrated mastery, but only of technique. Marian thought, It is not for me who have mastered nothing, and have no technique, to criticize this.

'You're very good,' she said to Violet, truthful up to a point only, returning downstairs.

'I sell,' said Violet. 'But the last thing you need is more pictures.'

Marian laughed. 'I haven't forgotten that you want one,' she said. 'And you will come out to dinner with me – shall we say next Tuesday? I'll come and fetch you.'

Alice had begun practising in an empty house. The viola part didn't stand up alone. She could always hear the other parts running in her head, weaving the pattern, and she could only dimly understand how the viola heard alone might strike a listener. It was a relief not to be listened to, however. She worked for an hour on her part in a Mozart quartet, and then moved on to playing a Bach piece for solo cello. That gave all the tune to her. Lovely, dark music.

She finished a slow movement, and realized suddenly that she was not, after all, alone. Leo had come in. He had come to the living-room door and stopped to listen. She would have been cross at his eavesdropping had he not said softly,

*Musing my way through a sombre and favourite fugue
By Bach who disburdens my soul, but perplexes my
fingers . . .*

'Gosh, Leo, what's that?' she said, startled.

'Sassoon.'

'Who?'

'Ah. Music's not the only art,' he said. 'There are cross-connections. He's a poet.'

'Can you remember more of it?'

'No; but I'll lend you the book if you like.'

'Yes I would.'

'Come and get it some time.'

'Did you want Mum?'

'Some other time will do,' he said, waving at her as he left.

Alone again, Alice decided to be useful – to cook a chowder for supper. She needed fresh scallops, and cod, and a crab to stand in for lobster. Also a potato-peeler – being left-handed she couldn't use her mother's. She liked shopping like this, going from shop to shop with a basket on her arm like a Victorian photograph. And she needed some soothing activity.

Later she was on her way home, up the long hill from the town. Halfway up was a little bric-a-brac shop with pretty things in the window. She hesitated, and then went in. Almost the largest item in the shop was a dark-red marble lamp, shaped like a lighthouse on a chunk of rock, polished, and sombrely gleaming. At first Alice thought she liked it, but she turned her back on it, studied, or pretended to study, a rack of Coalport plates, and tried to imagine the lamp carried home and lighting a corner of a natural room. It wouldn't, of course, shed much light, since the little torch bulb in its imitation lamp-chamber was too faint. It was a light to look at, not one to see by. Was it beautiful then? Enough to earn a place in a room? For it certainly wouldn't be useful. Alice had recently heard, from Max, William Morris's dictum, 'Have nothing in your house that you do not know to be useful, or believe to be beautiful,' and was trying to live by it. In the case of the potato peeler she had just acquired at Woolworths this was both clear and easy; in the case of a stone lighthouse?

She turned round, and looked at it again, perceiving it now as rather kitsch.

'Serpentine,' murmured the hovering lady in the back of the shop.

'I beg your pardon?' said Alice. The word caused a tremor of recognition.

'The lamp. It's made of serpentine,' the shopkeeper said.

'Oh – I didn't know serpentine was *stuff*,' said Alice.

'It's a Cornish rock,' the woman told her. 'Very popular. It ranges in colour from deep reds to deep greens. That piece is quite a rare one – it isn't often you get a large object made in the deepest red.'

'Local?' asked Alice. 'Do you know where?'

'On the Lizard. The other coast. There are craftsmen still working it there, but this piece, of course, is old. Sometime in the twenties, I think. It's signed on the base.'

'Are there caves?' asked Alice. She was almost holding her breath.

'That I don't know,' said the woman. 'Perhaps at Kynance? I think there are caves at Kynance.' But she was losing interest in Alice as Alice was visibly losing interest in the lamp.

She almost ran up the rest of the way to the house. Toby

was lounging in a fraying deck-chair in the back garden, on the only little scrap of level ground between the terraced flower-beds, the rampant fuchsia hedges. An inverted open book lay on his unbuttoned shirt. Alice dumped herself down beside him.

'Look, it isn't a winding cave, snaking around,' she said.

'What isn't, sister dear?'

'A serpentine cave – it means a cave in a kind of rock – there's a rock called serpentine!'

'O ho,' he said. 'Where?'

'There's serpentine at a place called Kynance. There might be caves there too.'

'Hang on while I get the map,' he said.

They spread the map out on the ground. 'Look, it isn't far at all,' he said. 'And someone at work recommended a good restaurant at Helston, pretty much on the way. Let's take mother out for the day, and treat her to dinner on the way back.'

'Can we afford that?' she asked. Musicians, he supposed, must be chronically short of money. Alice had no idea of the *scale* of extravagances – everything she couldn't afford was lumped together – fresh Colombian coffee beans, champagne, yachts on the Mediterranean, designer clothes, meals out, economy size boxes of detergent . . . He grinned at her.

'I can afford it,' he said serenely.

'Shall we tell her where we're going?' Alice wondered aloud.

'Let's surprise her,' said Toby.

'We'll take a picnic lunch, shall we?' Alice asked.

'If you like. I'll do dinner, you do lunch, OK?'

'Thursday?'

'Tomorrow would suit me better,' he said. 'I'm tied up Thursday.'

'How can you be tied up?' she asked him. 'Where are you going?'

'Fishing,' he said.

They had tried working it out over drinks in the Sloop – Toby felt it incumbent upon him to buy the round of drinks. He noticed with annoyance that he was trembling slightly in the aftermath of the confrontation, and hoped it wouldn't make him spill the beer.

'So how come you'm walking around impersonating Mathy?' asked the tall lad.

'I'm not impersonating anybody!' said Toby, indignant. 'I am just going about my own business. I was just born looking like this.'

'Well, quite right, that's the thing, idn it?' someone said.

'He must be your cousin, Matt,' suggested the girl. Ann, Toby thought. He was trying to learn names, fast.

'Don't know how, though,' said Matthew Huer. 'Wouldn' I know a thing like that?'

'Your ma would know,' said one of the young men – were they calling him Bass? One of the famous nicknames? 'Ask her, why don't you?'

'Well, she idn't here right now,' said Matt. 'Don't you know about it?' He addressed Toby, and added, 'My 'ansome,' to general laughter.

'I have a sort of missing grandfather,' said Toby. 'He must have been someone in your family, I suppose.'

''Ang on, Matt,' said a third boy. 'Afore we go asking the parents. We could be stirring things up.'

'I want to know, though,' said Matty. 'Gives me a shiver just to look at him.'

'I want to know too,' said Toby.

'Ess, that's natural,' said Bass.

'My grandmother was a painter,' offered Toby. 'She lived here for a while. And my mother was illegitimate, we suppose. She doesn't know who her father was. Our only clue is a painting. We were told it was of someone called Tremorvah. Thomas Tremorvah.'

'That's our mam's maiden name,' said Ann – Mathy's sister, Toby realized. 'But I never heard of any Thomas. Did you, Matt?'

He shook his head. 'No,' he said.

'But there must be a link between us somewhere,' said Toby. He found himself floundering, desperately hoping that this man was his cousin, that the pretty, narrow-faced, sharp-eyed Ann was kindred, as long as she wasn't too close.

'Can't be sure, in St Ives,' another man said. 'There be a lot of connections here. Lot of likenesses running around; lot of intermarriage. Mathy's grandad might be your grandad, and might be someone who looked like someone, see?'

'Can we ask your grandad?' said Toby.

'Dead,' replied Matt.

'Well, how much do they two look alike?' asked Bass. 'Let's have 'em side by side a minute.'

Toby and Matthew sat together on a high-backed pew. The others stood around staring. Finally Bass said, 'It's when they move around they do be closest. It's how they walk.'

'He looks much more like you than Jack does,' said Ann, decisively. 'That's our other cousin,' she said to Toby. He blessed her silently for the word 'other'.

'Do you want another beer, anyone?' he said, unwisely no doubt trying to placate the tribunal.

'Keep your money in your pocket. I'll get 'em,' said Matthew at once, standing up.

'Hey, Mathy!' said the man called Graham at Matthew's back, 'I've got a notion! Wadn't you wanting someone to go out with you Thursday? Fishing,' he said to Toby. 'Bass has to go to Trurer Thursday, and Matt is short-handed. If you be his cousin you oughter be able to do that for him, didn't you?'

'OK,' said Toby. 'Of course I will.' He could feel the tremor of amusement the moment he said it.

'There you are then, skipper,' said Bass, as Matthew came back with a tray of full glasses. He was grinning broadly.

It was a long way down the cliff to Kynance. From the car-park the track descended a steep little valley, with a tiny stream in the cleft. But Marian remembered something quite different – a cliff-face so steep it was perilous – she had been passed down it like a rucksack. She remembered the adult fear of falling, surrounding her like a feeling in the air. She herself had not been frightened. And the path they were now on, with Toby bounding ahead of her, was perfectly safe. True, they found it zigzagged steeply at the bottom, and finished in a scramble over boulders.

It seemed at first like simply a cove, a pretty cove. But as they walked further it unfolded – there was indeed a double strand, a spur of sand with the sea on both sides of it, with a looming grass-topped cliff-bound island at the further end. Standing in both sand and sea were towers of rock, a group of dark giants, so that they were reminded, all three of them, of the sense of being a tiny child, surrounded by the looming heights of adults. The sun was shining. 'Under the glassy clear, translucent waves,' said Alice's memory to her. She said it aloud, the words snatched away from her and tossed into incoherent snatches by the brisk wind.

'What, sib?' said Toby, turning towards her, blinking and shading his eyes, for she stood against the light, aureoled in it, as it sprang dazzling off the tossing water behind her. But she said only, 'Look,' and held out to him nested in her two hands an egg-shaped dark red stone, polished in the tumble of a little stream. Alice was standing in the bed of the stream, which was over her shoes, and soaking her socks. She was standing on green and red marbled pebbles, polished by the clear water. 'This is serpentine,' she said. 'It's lovely; look.'

'It's everywhere, all this – ' Toby waved at the standing monoliths around them. 'The roughness hides it – look at the foot of the stones, where the sea rubs the sand against them.'

Toby pulled off his shoes, and left them topping a boulder. They held hands, and waded into the dashing waves, pointing out to each other the smoothed sides of the rock, its rich colours which were hidden by the roughness and cracks above.

'It's a marvellous place,' said Toby. 'It must be the place she remembers – where is she?'

'Somewhere,' said Alice. 'Can't see her at the moment.'

Marian had wandered away, looking for her cave. She couldn't find it at first. She wandered out along the sand bar and stood for a few minutes staring amazed at the cleft in the rocks, in which the waves thumped, and then exploded sighing in a burst of upthrust spray. When she looked round the cave was behind her. The gleaming walls she remembered looking up at were now just a border, snaking along the sandy floor. Compared to the brilliant beach-light around her the cave was dark, though it gaped to the light. She stood looking into it till her eyes widened, till she could see the rocks. It was curious and potent; a pungent organic smell reeked from it – of weed and shell and watery decay; of fish and salt and sea-wrack. And it had an organic look to it too. Like a great gaping fistula in something living, it seemed to be lined with flesh, dark flesh like meat cut yesterday, a sanguinary sombre red, with white flecks and strands of tendon and gristle running in it, and a dull green bloom of fester spreading over it in patches. Marian shuddered, and stepped inside.

Facing her was another roughly polished wall of the same mortuary colours. Her child's eye, she thought, had rejected the words someone had spoken: 'Precious stones. Well, semi-precious.' Young Marian had seen the rocks as flesh. Now old Marian wondered where she had found such a morbid eye. And memory answered her. For in her precise generation children had seen things, it couldn't be helped, there had been death all around.

Where had it been? She and Stella had been staying somewhere . . . as usual, Marian didn't know where. The bomb had fallen on the house opposite. She was lying in bed, and she heard the little scratching sound made by fine debris skittering against the window, like mice behind the skirting. That always came first. Then the blast – a huge sound that rattled everything in the room, and hurt her ears, though she had slipped down the sheets, and her head was under the blankets, before it came. Last, a long aftermath of thumps and rumbles and crashes, as larger debris, thrown into the air varying distances, fell back. It was warm in the bed, and at first she did not move. Then she wriggled up again enough to emerge from the tunnel of bedding and put her head back on the pillow.

There was quiet, after the bomb. But gradually the room became colder, until it was very cold. A disturbing sensation reached her, as of the waft of the open air, the creeping secrets of the night garden. At last she got up, and padded barefoot to the window. Had it been there, but open, she would not have been able to close it without help; but it was not there. Where the window had been there was a neat rectangular hole in the wall, brightly moonlit. Marian fetched a chair from the corner of the room, placed it under the hole, climbed up on it, and looked out. The street looked like one of her drawings. The nursery schoolteacher gave her dark, blue-black sugar paper to crayon on, and everything you drew on it absorbed darkness, and showed faintly in pale outlines. As now the street did, under the unflinching moon.

The row of houses opposite had a new gap, as though it had lost a milk tooth. The bedroom window was lying on the front lawn, with some of the glass broken in the frame. To Marian's eye the flight of the window, and its alighting on the lawn, had no more reason than the inexplicable movements of the garden birds.

Beyond the supine window-frame, in the flower bed and on the pavement of the street beyond, were some giant broken dolls. Staring into the moonlight, in which every outline was furry, drawn in soft chalk, she made out an arm, palm upwards, a burst torso, and a leg. These things glistened in the dark light, with unfamiliar subcutaneous things, veins and bones exposed, under a surface that gleamed wet. On the garden path was lying a great doll in an attitude familiar to Marian. It had its arms raised above its head, and the skirt of its nightdress thrown up over its face, leaving legs and belly bare, and a faintly marked delicate fanny open to view. Marian's friend Michael loved to expose Marian's own doll, Amanda Virginia, in this way, and then point and giggle. 'She's rude!' he would say. 'Buy her some knickers!' Marian would be shocked, but would usually laugh, as she laughed then.

She was still laughing when the men in tin hats came running down the street. They looked at the dolls, and one of them pulled down the nightdress, uncovering its face. Then they came running into the house. They released her mother trapped in the back bedroom, the door of which was wedged solid by the fractional move- ment of the cracked house. One of them came into Marian's room, peeled the coverlet, and wrapped it round her. He picked her up and carried her downstairs to Stella, who was sitting shaking and weeping in a dusty armchair. He put Marian into her mother's arms.

'Unscathed,' he said.

And Marian had always thought that was true. She had not revisited the memory often, and never with the fierce freshness with which it came to her now, but she thought she had been unscathed. But wasn't it scathe which had made her see – which made her still see – the innocent rock as flesh?

She had felt fear, but nevertheless had walked towards the back of the cave, until the bright light from the other end drew her onwards. This is what she did now, advancing towards the gleaming rock. So vivid was the trace of memory that she felt the firm sand under her naked feet, the inaudible but tangible grind of minute golden grains against each other and against her skin.

'What did I do with my shoes?' she wondered, having forgotten taking them off, and where she put them – and looking down found she was still wearing them; it was the remembered self that had gone barefoot.

There was a place in the crook of the cave where you could see out of it both ways. Marian stood there, wondering how she had been trapped. Had the sea closed both mouths? Perhaps at high tide it did – yes, obviously, because she was standing on firmly founded sand, cemented by the secretion of the sea. Puzzled, she walked out of the further entrance – she had to duck her head – onto the sand bar beyond. It was a wide beach now, with waves breaking softly on each side of it. And surely this was the place – there was the chunk of cliff that would be islanded when the tides came in and the waves met. What would they look like, breaking into each other like opposing armies? Had she lingered too long, looking? She must have had a child's lack of sense, then, for any adult could see that there was no other way onto this stretch of sand, the path through the cave being the only way once the tide advanced. Perhaps as a very little child she had not realized.

Marian turned back through the cave. She was half in the present, going to find her children, one of whom had a rucksack with picnic food. And as she walked in the gloom of the cave the light at its mouth struck her. She blinked, dazzled. And she saw the sunlit water breaking white, and on the shining sand in the cave's mouth bodies lying. They had been as naked as the poor broken dolls, but they were not dead. They moved; they struggled and heaved, and gasped. They were lumbering like beached seals against each other, skin to skin. Under the woman's head her discarded dress was lying across the sand. The bright light danced on the printed pattern of pansies and leaves. She cried like a mewing gull.

And Marian had been frightened and run away. She had run back through the cave, and out onto a ribbon of sand to be engulfed by the rising waters.

And this was what she had forgotten. Clean forgotten, wiped out of mind. So that only now, at this moment of recollection, could she see the scathe; the fear of drowning in an invisible sea which had made her clench her teeth and her fists, made her cringe and feel slimy as a seal, made Donald, poor Donald, call her frigid. He hadn't known the half of it; had never known why if he managed to bring the wave to breaking point he had to hold her closely all night long, had to console her for the inflicted joy. He held her without knowing where she was – but she had been on a black rock cut off, cut off from land, and shivering in the arms of a stranger.

And most painfully, acutely, she asked herself how could Stella have done that? How could she have let that happen? Marian would have suffered any loss, any delay of yearned for encounters, rather than leave one of her children wandering in a place of danger while she put herself beyond recall, beyond the reach of appeal, the duty of care thrown utterly aside. And it cast Stella, she saw at once, in quite a new unfavourable light. However often in her heart she had felt neglected in the cause of art, it was quite different to be – to have been – endangered for the sake of lust; for the sake of a hasty grapple on the sands. She needed to find Stella and yell at her, reproach her, vent her anger, extort some kind of explanation, some kind of apology, any kind of acknowledgement that she, Marian, mattered too – mattered enough to have been looked after, to have been kept from harm, and from untimely knowledge. From the sight of death no loving care could have kept her, in those days, but from that other knowledge of the nature of the flesh she should have been protected.

And this justified indignation, like so much else, had come too late; death had foreclosed it. Marian took a deep breath, and walked out again onto the sunlit landward beach, where Toby and Alice could be seen a little way off, perched, picnic at the ready, on top of a knoll of rock, waving her towards them. In Alice's slender extended hands the smooth serpentine pebbles were held out for her admiration, and she managed, shuddering briefly, shaking off the feeling of the cave, to see them as, and call them, pretty stones. Cold stones, harmless, patient, pleasing things. Their roundness was wholeness. Alice had weighed herself down with them, filling her rucksack with their dead weight, choosing them out and caressing them one by one.

Marian sat in the sun, beside the bright tumult of the waters, and ate her lunch. The three of them, out together on a jaunt, as they had done when Toby and Alice were children. It was different, though; Marian, who had usually been calm and motherly, concentrating on being motherly, now mused silently on herself at every pause in the talk. Toby, who had been the restless one, running about and climbing trees, now stretched out on a rug at her side, quite peaceful. Alice was sad, playing with her pebbles and spreading cheese on biscuits, and talking, distracting herself, disguising sadness, but not succeeding. Marian wondered whether to ask Alice what was wrong, but would not do so now, on this bright and riotous shore, which the children had found and brought her to, as a gift, in the hope of pleasing her. Very well, then, she would be pleased. By and by she would paddle, playing with the ambushing surge of surf, and eating an apple as she walked. Her children would laugh and join her, and all would be well.

So it was. They brought home as many chunks of serpentine as they could lug up the steep to the car-park, and made a cairn in the garden.

'There is a problem, Toby,' Marian said. They were having drinks in the porch, watching the dusk, while Alice, austerely audible from the living room, played her viola. It was a dark and grinding sort of sound she was making – steady and urgent as a heartbeat. Like a heartbeat it sounded at once indispensable and subordinate to some other, greater thing. Listening to it spread a kind of unease through the house, a sense of something taken apart that should have been kept together, of something dissected alive, tremulous, shivering.

'Stella seems to have owed Leo money, and I gather from the lawyer's letters that there isn't any. The last letter is on my desk – look at it if you like. You don't happen to know if we are liable for debts incurred by your grandmother, do you?'

'Her estate would be. You personally, no. I think. I'm not an expert. But it isn't down to legalities, is it? Rather a question of keeping Gran's promises? How much is it?'

'Ten thousand. He says he was doing something for her. To be honest when he first turned up I thought he was some kind of blackmailer.'

Toby laughed. 'Threatening to tell the world what, exactly? About Gran's respectable past?'

Marian laughed too.

'I think he's just eccentric,' said Toby. 'He's quite straight, I think.'

'What's worrying me, really, is that I wouldn't have thought Stella would incur a debt without some way of paying it.'

'But she did it all the time!' he said.

'Not in this way. Endless confusion, endless things forgotten, living hand-to-mouth – we all know what she was like. But commissioning something from a fellow artist – an old friend and pupil – which she could not possibly pay for?'

'What was it?'

'He says "a work". I haven't seen it, or asked about it. I'm going up to London tomorrow to see the lawyer. He has found me some art dealer to look at the paintings, so I shall try to settle things at Barrington while I'm at it.'

'Your famous orderly mind coming in handy at last!' he said. 'Poor Ma. Shall I come with you?'

'Only if you want to,' she said.

Toby lay on his back on his bed, his hands linked behind his head on the pillow. He lay in darkness, listening to the rattle of his window in the wind from the sea. He had told his mother that Leo was straight, as though he felt expert on the detection of straightness or crookedness in other people. But the truth was, he thought ruefully, that if he had been as good at it as all that he should have been better at looking after himself. He had made a big mistake trusting that girl. The trouble was, you needed greedy people to deal in big money. The greedy people were alert and clever at spotting the moment – it might literally be

a moment – when they should buy or sell. They got –
Toby got – an immense buzz out of winning in the endless
battle of wits, out of squeezing gains from the money as
it flowed round the world. Clever people made money
whichever way things went, like those turbo generators
that got energy from both falling and rising tides. And
some of them didn't have the instinct for honesty. You
couldn't get that from reading the Companies Acts. And
anyway, what was being done by the insider traders would
have been well within the law a few years back. Back then,
making use of scraps of gossip, passing scraps of gossip to
friends, was just what was done. Only outsiders and fools
lost by it. It's hard to have instinctive revulsion for something that used to be perfectly legal and widespread. It's
stupid to pass unenforceable laws. The larger the sums of
money involved, the more likely it is that the victim is a
huge corporation trying a take-over bid. The less likely
that the savings of little old ladies have gone down the
spout.

Toby had ridden this train of thought before. But he
didn't like the destination. He didn't know if it was
possible to prosper and make money for the company
while keeping honour bright. He was very sure that his
masters didn't give a fuck for honesty; they had not
suspended employees and started an enquiry from hatred
of dishonesty; they had done it to cover their backs, and
find out who to sack for the stupidity of breaking the rules
visibly enough to draw attention to the operation. But he
himself had not had an unerring enough sense. What
he had done that seemed only slightly tricky at the time,
could plainly be seen, with hindsight, to have been wrong.
He felt now, about going back to dealing, like someone
who has made one very bad error of navigation, being put
back in charge of plotting a course for a ship. And he was

unused to self-loathing; he had always had plenty of self-esteem.

He groaned and sat up, to stare at the window. He could see a muted brightness behind the dark scud of the clouds. He had wanted money badly. Lots of money. He had wanted independence – freedom to live wherever he liked, work at whatever he liked. He had wanted to make a fortune by the time he was thirty. He had been one of the greedy people. He had overheard a single enigmatic remark, and based on it made a brilliant guess. He had been so absolutely right that it looked like a real leak, really inside inside knowledge. And that sort of guess had been contaminated by some of his colleagues. If you wanted independence, he realized, one way was making a lot of money; another way would be to need very little, and keep your nose clean.

He was thinking, of course, of Matthew.

It had at least been a calm day. Flat calm, or so he had thought, clambering down the granite steps from the quay to the deck of Matthew's boat. But as soon as they rounded the quay the boat began to buck and dip on an unbreaking ground swell that had been invisible from the shore, at least to Toby's uninformed eye. White wings of foam spread and folded rhythmically under the prow. The little boat didn't ride like the yachts Toby had sailed, but butted straight through, getting knocked about by the water. There was a grinding sound from the engine, and a smell of engine-oil and fish. Toby was wearing bright yellow waterproof overalls, Matthew's second pair, a bit too large for him. Matthew stood at the wheel in the little cabin and set a course that swung round the Island, and past Porthmeor Beach. The town shone at them in the bright light – the white Tate, the grey flock of headstones in the cemetery, the glinting windows of the house rows. Beyond the grey tumbled boulders on Clodgy Point, however, the land was dark; the facing cliffs cast into shadow by the morning sun. The deck bucked under Toby's feet, and his sense of speed disorientated him; they left a churning white trail of wake, and seemed to be speeding in the water, but the folded and broken panorama of shadowy cliff moved only slowly past them.

Before they reached the lobster pots Toby was feeling queasy. It was hard work. The rope ran over a rusty windlass, turned by hand, yanking the heavy sodden pots out of the water. Most were empty; Toby had to put a chunk of fish into each one, and throw it back. It sank away from him into the glassy depth, disappearing in a trail of bright bubbles, and he hauled up the next one. There were some lobsters – little ones, but saleable, Matthew said. There were some crabs. And there were some crawfish, which Matthew said were dandy eating. Toby laboured, turning the winch handle, heaving the pots around, aching in every muscle. Matthew, having dropped anchor by the pot lines, and run up the mizzen sail to head them up into the wind, stood by, talking, and telling Toby what to do. Toby could see he was being put upon, and gritted his teeth. He could by will-power keep from stopping work, but could not help his breakfast spewing suddenly on the deck. He was folded in two, retching. Matthew grinned, heaved a bucket of sea onto the deck and swilled the vomit overboard.

'Not many more,' he said. He began to lend a hand, doing some of the lifting, while Toby wound the winch.

They worked on for what seemed like another age. Then suddenly the last pot had been baited and slung overboard. Matthew fetched up a thermos of hot tea, and when Toby shook his head, insisted.

'Caan't take ee in looking green, boy,' he said. 'Caan't 'ave it seem as though I've been aworking you *'aard.*'

Toby drank the hot black tea, and ate a bite of something called 'a heavy' – a dense yellow bun that more than lived up to its name. It was kill or cure; it would settle his stomach or come back up again at once, he supposed. He tried to take his mind off it by asking questions.

'Is there a living in fishing, Matthew?'

'Ess. Yes; if you don't be greedy. Depends what you mean by a living. Not what *you'd* call a living, maybe.'

'So what's a living according to you?'

'Well, I got a cottage in Downalong. Belongs to an uncle of mine. I can get by. Now if I was to start wanting a big car . . .'

'What about a girlfriend?'

'I can get along with a St Ives girl. Couldn't afford an up-country girl, but then I wouldn't want to.'

'Where does up-country start?' asked Toby. He probably wasn't going to be sick again.

'East'ards of the Bar,' said Matthew. 'Scillies is all right. Likewise over to Penzance. But going with someone east-'ards of the Bar means trouble. That's what Gran says. I go by what my Gran says.'

'Where's the Bar?' asked Toby, nearly sure he was being sent up.

'Hayle Bar,' said Matthew. 'About five miles up-country. Anything this side of that'll do. Let's go along in now. Wind's freshening. It'll be coming rough.'

When the boat started moving again he gave the wheel to Toby. They butted their way through the swell. The

town came into sight again, a spatter of whites and greys
and ochres and bright glinting windows spread out along
the shadowy landmass, below the steeple on the hill
behind it. They chugged along past the sweep of surf
breaking on Porthmeor, and the white complex shape of
the Tate.

'Preferred the gasworks, myself,' said Matthew.

'I like it,' said Toby, abandoning diplomacy, feeling
comfortable with Matthew.

'Outside's better'n what's in it, I'll give you that,' said
Matthew.

'What about the Alfred Wallises?' asked Toby. 'He was
a St Ives man, wasn't he? Painted seine fishing and things?
Don't you like him?'

'Not a lot,' said Matthew. 'I'll tell you a thing about
him. My auntie used to live across the yard from him. She
uster cook a hot dinner for him now and then – he was a
poor broken down old man at that time – and he would
give her a picture each time. Know what she did? She used
to chop them up for kindling, and put them by the stove
ready. The value of the gift was as kindling. Now there
do be two in there!' He gestured over the gunwale
towards the fast disappearing Tate.

'What do you like?' asked Toby.

'I like what my Gran 'as,' said Matthew. 'She got a
lovely picture of the sea by Mr Olson over the mantelpiece, and a nice one of the harbour by Mr Park over the
sideboard in the back room. I like both them.' Toby was
silenced, not having heard of either artist, and fearing the
worst.

As they passed the Island, looking stark and rocky from
the outer side, for it turned its soft green slopes inland,
Matthew took the wheel. He swung them offshore, giving
a wide berth to the rocky point, and took them gently into

harbour. They nosed up to the steps at the end of the quay, and carried the boxes of catch up the steps.

A reception committee of grinning young men awaited them.

''Ow d'you get on, Mathy?' asked Bass.

'He'll do,' said Matthew.

Toby said, stiff with up-country politeness, 'Thank you, Matthew, I enjoyed that.'

And Matthew said, ''Ang on, you idn't done yet. You be coming to see my Granny.'

How remote St Ives is depends whether you measure by miles or by hours. An early morning train gets you into London by two. There is plenty of time to think on such a journey.

Marian took a taxi from Paddington to the lawyer's offices. This was a shabby building at a smart address. The Dickensian smell of old documents seeped into the waiting room from the yawning spaces beyond. The rooms had once been grand and well proportioned; now they were divided by frosted glass screens into depressing tall cubby holes. Marian had to wait before being ushered into the carpeted and undivided warmth of a partner's office, a worn leather armchair facing the desk, and the offer of a cup of coffee.

The lawyer – he had come to Stella's funeral – shuffled papers on the desk. He looked ill at ease. He would greatly prefer, no doubt, to announce large unexpected fortunes to astonished legatees; Marian knew he could have no such duty this afternoon.

'I'm afraid I have bad news for you, Mrs Easton,' he said.

'How bad?' Marian asked.

'It could be worse, to be honest with you,' he said glumly. 'She has left no debts. It's almost as if she had calculated to the nearest penny how far she could go, but her affairs were in such disorder I can hardly believe—'

'She never did any calculating that I am aware of,' said Marian, musing, 'and yet . . . she did very greatly value her independence. She would have calculated any looming threat to that.'

'Well, to put you in the picture. There are no less than three mortgages on the house. When it has been sold, assuming it can be sold at valuation, there will be just enough equity left in it to cover transaction costs, and the small bequest to the Lifeboat Institution. We have found some money, in a building society account that has not been touched for fifteen years, that will discharge the remaining debts, but there will be nothing left, I am afraid, for the main beneficiaries – that is for you and your children. I am so sorry.'

'We were not expecting money,' said Marian. 'Except – she had incurred a debt of honour, for a sum of ten thousand pounds, that I thought she might have made some provision for.'

'I'm afraid testamentary law doesn't work like that. All the assets are balanced against all the debts. There's a precedence of claims. Of course, if there were a surplus, it would be up to you—'

'But there isn't.'

'Alas, no. You do inherit her chattels, her furniture and effects, that sort of thing.'

'Well, her furniture . . .'

'No fine antiques?'

'All very old and battered. Perfectly serviceable, but . . . What about her paintings?'

'Well, painting, would certainly be effects,' he said, cheering up. 'But it seems that they are all there is.'

'There's a real appropriateness to that,' Marian told him.

Matthew's Granny lived a long way up the town, at a place called Penbeagle. Matthew went first to Stevens's fish shop, just behind the harbour, and bought a mackerel for his Gran's tea. 'If she asks if I catched it, and I say ess, hold your face still and don't say different,' Matthew said. Toby trudged up the steeply sloping road beside Matthew, through the Victorian terraces – the town had exploded in size when the railway reached it, to judge by the architecture – past the Leach Pottery and the fire station, and right at the top they found themselves in a spreading colony of bungalows and little houses, a council estate.

'How does your Gran come to be living up here,' asked Toby, 'so far away from you?'

'Council,' said Matthew. 'They condemned the house she was in, and rehoused her up here. And now that house she uster 'ave belongs to a teacher from Birmingham. All fancied up. It's empty half the year.' He opened the glazed plastic door – it didn't seem to be locked – and the two young men stepped in.

'Gran?' Matthew called. 'I've hooked him and fetched him up here, along of this bit of mackerel.'

'Put him in the best room a minute, Mathy,' said a voice from the back. Toby stepped into the living room. Flowery wallpaper; a glass-fronted cupboard with china plates, and some trophies; on top of it a row of photographs. School photos of smiling children – one of them recognizably of Mathy; it could easily have been of Toby himself. Some graduates wearing gowns and holding scrolls; someone on top of a mountain. A print of *The Light of the World* framed in gilt hung over the sofa; and over the gas fire a painting of boats in the harbour – to Toby's eye a surprisingly good painting, academic and expert, and rather good at a certain kind of late afternoon light. He was staring at the signature, trying to decipher it when Mathy carried in a tray of tea, and his Gran came padding behind him in bulging carpet slippers.

'Let's be looking at ee, then,' she said.

A thin old lady with a dowager's hump, peering at him. She must have been a tall woman, because even crooked with age, she didn't have to look up to him much. She had very dark eyes, like Mathy's, like his own. She was wearing a soft hand-knitted cardigan and a silky blouse with an agate brooch at the neck. She took her time.

Then, 'Ess,' she said. 'You do be like a Vanson.'

'What's a Vanson?' asked Toby.

'I am,' said Matthew's Gran. 'Mrs Bessie Vanson. And so is Mathy – Matthew Vanson.'

'I thought you were Mathy Huer?' said Toby, blinking.

'That's my nickname,' said Mathy. 'Huer. There's maybe four or five Matthew Vansons in St Ives. I'm Huer, and then there's Bass – that's my uncle; and then there's Tommy Dolphin, that's my cousin, and my other cousin's called Bounder, and—'

'Don't run on, Mathy,' said Mrs Vanson. 'Have him sit down and I'll pour tea.'

The tea was strong and black, and served with some very dense yellow buns – more 'heavies', no doubt. Toby ate and drank, and his eyes wandered to the photograph.

'That was about when Mathy got called Huer,' Mrs Vanson said, following his glance. 'He talked about the pilchards coming back. My doing. I was always talking about it, though it was down to nearly nothing when I could remember. My mother remembered them taking in millions, and bringing them through the streets in cartloads. Lovely old times, she said. I'd like to have seen it. The Huer used to watch for the shoals coming into the bay, see.'

'You never saw a pilchard, I suppose?' said Toby.

'Only in a tin,' said Mathy.

'Now then,' said Mrs Vanson. 'What we have to work out is, where you come in the family. I'd like to have that cleared up before we have wild rumours running about.'

'The trouble is, that I don't know,' Toby told her. 'My Gran was Stella Harnaker. She was a painter, and she worked here for a bit. But we just don't know who our grandfather was. We have an oil-painting of him – or of someone, rather, that we think might be him. And a friend has told us that the picture is of someone called Tremorvah. Thomas Tremorvah.'

'Well, there is Tremorvahs related to us,' said Mrs Vanson. 'Related by marriage, that is. But I thought I should know of all the childer there ever was of that branch. What was your mother's name?'

'Marian.'

'I never head of any Marian Tremorvah.'

'I don't think my grandparents were married. My mother is called Marian Harnaker. Well, Marian Easton since her marriage. Perhaps it was all hushed up.'

'Well, I do remember there was some talk once. Something to do with Tremorvahs. But you're going back more'n fifty years, now. Half the people who might know a thing are gone. Now here's a question for you, my handsome. If there was something to cover over, do you want to know it? If your mother arose from someone doing what they shouldn't?'

'Well, *I'd* like to know how come I got a lick-spitting double, walking around the town, confusing people,' said Mathy.

'Maybe you would, Mathy boy, but I'm asking 'im.'

'I think my mother would like to know,' said Toby. 'I think not knowing has been hard on her. She thinks now she should have asked before Stella died. I can't think why she didn't.'

'Well, maybe she didn't like to,' said Mrs Vanson. 'I can't say as I would have liked to in her place. You young cocks live in such a wicked world you don't understand it. But in my generation we knew shame. Now, the person to ask is Mathy's other grandmother. Tremorvahs is that side of the family. And if you don't mind I'll talk to her myself, before sending you. Just in case she doesn't like it. You leave me a day or two, and I'll let you know. All right now?'

'Thank you. Quite all right,' said Toby. As they got up to leave, Mrs Vanson said, 'Thank you for my supper, Mathy.' And to Toby she said, 'He catches a good mackerel, that boy.'

'More mackerel than pilchards, anyway,' said Toby, straight-faced.

'It must feel very odd,' said Alice to Toby. She was cutting his toast into fingers for him to dip in his boiled egg. They were lingering over breakfast in their mother's absence, perceptibly released from some kind of unspoken expectation about when meals will be, and how long they will take.

'Not having one's appearance for one's exclusive use?' he said. 'Yes, it does. It makes everything else about me feel rather provisional.'

'Because it could have been otherwise? It could have been otherwise for anybody, I suppose.'

'Yes. I could look like me, and be Matthew—'

'And he could look like himself and be you—'

'So what you look like and who you are are separate propositions, suddenly.'

'Unnerving. It would be horrible if you didn't like Matthew.'

'Luckily I do like him, rather a lot. Although he isn't the sort of person I would have expected to like.'

'Not clever enough for you?'

'He's not clever enough to be having my sort of problems,' said Toby bitterly. 'Or perhaps I mean not stupid enough. Either way, I envy him.'

'You don't; not really. He hasn't got any money, and you—'

'I what?'

'Can't see the point of anything else. You take after Dad.'

'I bloody don't!' said Toby indignantly. 'I'm here, aren't I?'

'Sorry I spoke,' said Alice. 'Darling brother, you're going to have to get all that straightened out, you know.'

Marian took the train to Royston and got a taxi. Darkness fell as the train rattled onwards, and it was raining when she arrived at the house. It seemed to have got dark early, and to be sharply cold compared to Cornwall, and the house, empty and unheated, felt bleak and damp. It was full of the days they had spent there waiting for Stella to die; Marian felt suddenly dejected. She should not have come back alone – she didn't have enough freeboard for it. Shivering, she plodded across the green to find supper and warmth in the pub.

Later she came in, and went through to the barn, still wearing her coat. She reached for the electric light switch, and then stopped. Moonlight fell through the huge window, and faintly made visible the shadowy stacks of paintings that were her inheritance. Darkening and brightening behind scudding clouds it showed her, propped on the easel, the shadowy face of Thomas Tremorvah, just discernible, staring at her out of the past. She turned away. His visage haunted her troubled sleep in the cold bedroom, the unaired bed.

Things look better in the morning. It had stopped raining, and Marian went for a brisk walk, and bought fresh coffee in the village shop, and a packet of biscuits to offer vestigial hospitality to the art dealer who was coming at eleven. She looked round the house to find, if she could, bits and pieces worth keeping, before the house was cleared. There wasn't much; even less than she had expected, only some pretty glasses and a few plates. It wasn't only that things just didn't stick to Stella, it was that she destroyed things – mixed paints on plates as temporary palettes and forgot to clean them, left dud batteries in the bedside radio until they spewed corrosive effusion that destroyed the plastic casing – inflicted every sort of dere-liction that neglect could accomplish. Whimsically,

Marian collected one or two battered and spattered objects as eloquent souvenirs – for herself, for the children – and was delicately wrapping ruined things and packing them into a cardboard box when the doorbell rang.

The dealer was smartly dressed, and spoke in a classy drawl. He introduced himself, 'James Gennyflower, call me James,' and accepted the offer of coffee. Marian disliked him a good deal by the time they reached the door to the barn.

'This will take me a little while,' he said, putting down his briefcase beside the easel, and producing a clipboard and a pen. 'Would you like to leave me to it?'

Marian wandered out into the chilly garden. Mildewed clumps of asters struggled in the rampant flower-beds. How vulgar Stella would think it to have paintings *valued*! But hadn't she priced them somehow, herself, when she wanted to sell them? Instinct answered Marian at once, that Stella would have known the difference between a price and a value; no doubt the price was more related to the pocket of the buyer than to the nature of the picture. Not that there had been many buyers. 'We do have to get probate, Mother,' she told Stella's lingering aftermath.

'Call me James' took over two hours in the barn. He emerged with dusty hands and a dishevelled appearance. It was half-past one, and there was not a bite to eat in the house. Marian suggested the pub, but declined to accompany him.

'I'm not through, I'm afraid,' he said. 'I'm expecting to take the rest of the day.'

Marian withdrew to the living room, and began to make phone calls and write letters, arranging for the phone to be disconnected, the meters read, the bills sent down to Cornwall. When she had done all she could think of she moved on to dealing with the clutch of bills from her house in Hull sent on to her by the colleague who rented two upstairs rooms from her there. Marian knew where she was with a gas bill. She had never lived beyond her means. Even the leave of absence without pay from the chemist's shop where she worked could be afforded without trouble. Donald had been generous to her financially, and her needs were modest. So now, she ordered her estate, and the residue of her mother's, and hoped for the comfort such a tiny triumph over chaos usually brought her, and did not find it. Without Stella's example to traduce, her competence had lost its *schadenfreude*.

It was half-past six before 'Call me James' emerged from the barn, more dishevelled than ever, and said, 'Right, I'm ready to report to you now. I'll send a written report, of course, but I expect you'd like to hear the gist. Let me take you out to dinner. The Pink Geranium used to be good. On me. I insist.'

Over pink tablecloths, then, and pink candles in silver candlesticks, and delicate portions of exquisite food and wine, which James had ordered for both of them with minimum consultation with his guest, he began to talk about Stella's pictures.

'Someone has sorted them out for you already,' he said.

'Leo Vincey.'

'Do you know Vincey?' He looked and sounded impressed.

'He was a friend of my mother's.'

'Of course; he's a St Ives man, isn't he? I would very much like to meet him.'

'Is he good?'

'I think so. He's controversial. Some would say now Hepworth is dead he must be the leading British sculptor, but he isn't a pile of bricks man. Not a dustbin lid and

jerrican man. He's a craftsmanly worker. Very unfashion-
able. But I admire him.'

'But I thought he was a painter—'

'Both. He does both. Now, your mother's work. She
hasn't a front line reputation, as I'm sure you know. But
there is a sort of interest by association in any painter who
worked in St Ives during the war years.'

'I know so little about it.'

'Well, you've heard of Ben Nicholson. Bryan Winter?
John Wells? Patrick Heron? Bernard Leach? Barns-
Graham? You knew that Hepworth worked in St Ives?
OK, look, I'll give you a bird's eye view in a nutshell . . .'

Marian laughed, and James laughed too.

'There's wonderful light down there.'

'I do know that,' Marian said.

'It had been an art colony for a long time. The war
displaced people, and brought refugees to England from
all over Europe. They had a very cosmopolitan view of
things. They gathered in London, at first, and then when
the blitz started some of them went to St Ives. Naum Gabo
for instance. Nicholson and Hepworth. There was a
hugely influential melting pot of ideas simmering away
down there. Nicholson was deeply influenced by Alfred
Wallis, a local primitive artist – you've heard of him?'

'Yes, I have,' said Marian.

'They all influenced each other deeply. And they quarrelled. There was a prolonged struggle with traditional
artists about hanging modern works in the art shows, and
some of the moderns split off and founded their own
society – the Penwith. But almost at once they were at
each other's throats again and the Penwith split again—'

'It's not a very edifying story, then.'

'No, not really. Now the point of all this is that your
mother was among them, painting. And what she painted

while she was in that circle, open to those influences, is very interesting. You can trace the effect of that artist and the other artist – she was struggling to paint something which took account of the new ideas while still being recognizably in the older tradition. They don't have much value in themselves, you understand, because there isn't much of a market in very minor modern artists, but they have a historical interest, and there are collectors of St Ives school paintings. We might try putting them on show as a group and seeing if we could nudge her reputation up a notch or two.'

'What about the others?'

'No good, I'm afraid. She had something when she was there, she was beginning to get something quite individual, something right on the cusp, and then she lost it. She reverted to form if you like; and the form she reverted to had been overtaken. It's an absolute calamity that she left St Ives. You don't know why she left, do you?'

Marian shook her head.

'After the war constructivist and abstract art took over, and the vanguard moved to New York.'

'Would she have known, do you think, that she had taken a wrong turning?'

'I can't tell you that. People often get this wrong, I think. There's a tendency to call artists derivative when they influence each other, and yet the influences can produce wonderful things. Cross-fertilization would be a better word, I think.'

While they talked Marian's idea of him had been changing. No doubt he was in the art business to make money; but it was also for love. He knew his subject. And what was wrong with her, that she should so instantly take a dislike to enthusiasts of any kind? He pulled a notebook from his pocket, and put it down beside his coffee cup.

'This is the low-down,' he said. 'There is a little pot of gold for you, because there are three Wallises. Worth around ten thousand each. There is also a Nicholson, worth about thirty thousand. You might get a few hundred apiece for the better St Ives canvases, if we get a gallery to show them together, and write them up a bit. The rest are worthless. In money terms, I mean.'

'I'm going to take some as mementoes, and ask you to deal with the rest,' said Marian.

'Your decision, of course. What you keep might appreciate, but I wouldn't hold my breath.'

'Why is Wallis so valuable?' Marian asked. 'I've heard people be very rude about him.'

'I don't think I can tell you that,' said James. 'But you might be able to see it if you looked. Go and look in Kettle's Yard.'

'Where's that?' asked Marian.

'Just down the road, in Cambridge,' he told her.

Alice was looking for Leo's house. She got lost in Downalong every time she walked there, and usually enjoyed the experience, but this time it was wet and windy. She asked three people, all of whom were tourists, and at least one of whom was lost herself. At last she found it – a sort of cellar door, down three steps and under an overhanging balcony, all up an unnamed sideways alley off a tiny steep street. A fancy pottery house label called it The Fish Cellar, but when Leo let her in, without comment – he had not been expecting her – it seemed to be the upstairs of the house, because a narrow stair led down. The room they were standing in contained a kitchen sink, a disintegrating armchair, and a television set, standing on a bare boarded floor.

'I've come to see you,' said Alice.

'I'm working,' said Leo.

'OK, I'll wait.'

'Come down, then,' he said. He was brusque, not his usual provocative roughness, but really. She followed him down. It should have been a below-ground basement, but it wasn't. The lower floor opened at the back into a large workshop, and the workshop had a set of French windows from wall to wall, giving onto a steep garden, falling away further, and with a view across to the far side of the bay, where the holiday camps were. At the foot of the stairs against the underground wall, beneath a sloping skylight that might have been a coal-chute once, and was now closed with very dirty glass, was an unmade bed, with a sagging curtain rail round it. There was a curtain, but it was pulled back, leaving the crumpled bed in view.

Leo immediately returned to a bench with an array of strange tools, chisels and mallets and scrapers. He was apparently at work sharpening something on a grindstone worked by a treadle under the bench. It made an unpleasant whine of varying pitch.

Alice took in, and was aware of her amazement at, the state of the workshop. Apart from the bed it was immaculately tidy. A chart chest stood in one corner, lacking its drawers, and full of sheets of paper. A shelf held a row of jars in which carefully assorted brushes stood like arrows in quivers. An amazing device hanging overhead like an old fashioned airer held arrays of tubes of paint, in processions of graded colours, slotted in by their caps, as in a toothpaste holder. A row of palettes hung on the wall. Leo's pictures were stacked like gramophone records, sideways on in sectioned bins beneath the workbench. There was not one on show.

At the far end of the workshop disorder had crept in. There was a table thickly plastered with gobbets of terracotta clay. A claggy turntable stood at one end of it. There was no work at this end of the workshop either, but a large crate was standing on a platform in the middle of the floor.

'Since you're here, you can help me open this,' said Leo.

'However did you get that down the stairs?' asked Alice. The crate was eight feet or so long, and both tall and deep.

'Through the yard gate, and those doors,' said Leo. Alice saw that above the crate on the ceiling was a sort of gantry, an overhead steel beam with a pulley and chains running on it. The crate had been manoeuvred into place with that.

'What do I do?' asked Alice.

Leo gave her a cold chisel, and said, 'I'm going to lever the lid up. You lever the other end. Gently.'

It took some time to get the lid off. Time enough for Alice to spot and read the label on the far end of the crate: Rogers Parsons and Sons. Tilbury. Bellfounders. Lifting the lid revealed nothing but swathes of bubble pack and wood-shavings. Leo proceeded to lever off the ends of the crate, and then detach the side panels from the base. He worked methodically with great care, issuing directions to Alice, whose role was to keep parts of the crate from springing back when they were prised open. She did as she was asked, having recognized Leo's extraordinary tension; he was strung up like her quartet just before a performance.

When the crate was completely dismantled, the chains and pulleys which had positioned it were tugged out of the way against the wall, and Leo began to remove the packaging. The wood shavings, smelling faintly of Christmas trees, spilled out across the floor. The bubble pack was tackled with an ivory paper-knife. Alice picked up a knife from the tool bench, and Leo bellowed at her, 'Nothing sharp!'

At last everything was unfixed, and Leo reached out both hands, and pulled the packing away. A bronze wave. What he uncovered was a bronze wave. It rose from its rectangular base whale-backed, and curved over, captured in the moment of breaking, with a hollow vortex under the crest. At one end the wave was peaking, with an almost cutting edge, at the other the avalanche of foam was spilling expansively. Leo had gone very still. He was standing in an intense sort of trance. Alice had been looking for some time before she saw, in the tunnel formed by the wave-crest, an exiguously moulded shape – the shape of a nearly submerged human figure.

Leo was pacing round, looking from every angle. 'Well?' he said suddenly.

'Did you make this, Leo? I don't know what to say—'

'It isn't finished.'

'Isn't it?'

'It needs fettling. And burnishing.'

'It's beautiful.'

'Glad you like it. Since it's yours. Or, Marian's, rather. Or Stella's, really. Stella wanted it.'

Suddenly, awkwardly, Leo began to cry, wiping away tears with angry strokes of the back of his hands.

'Oh, Leo, I know!' said Alice, putting her arms round him. He went absolutely rigid.

'Don't touch me,' he said. 'Do you know how like Stella you are? As she was, long ago . . . I can't answer for myself if you touch me.'

'It's all right, Leo,' said Alice, 'I'm a grown-up. I'll answer for both of us.'

Kettle's Yard turned out to be a house – well, barely more than a cottage, really. Someone's house, filled with paintings and sculpture and bequeathed to the university. The tiny rooms were painted white, and had rather minimum furniture. Arrangements of beach pebbles lay on battered tables. And there were pictures on every available wall, even in the bathroom.

At first Marian didn't quite get it – the crudely painted boards and scraps of card which Wallis had covered with sea scenes seemed out of key with the sophisticated works, with the Nicholson abstracts, the lovely engraved Perspex shape by Naum Gabo, the Wyndham Lewis in the attic. Then in the extension to the house there was a whole wall of Wallises – a dozen or more. And there the dream ships voyaged on remembered storms, with stiff sails and chugging funnels, quite out of perspective and setting their courses in the mind's eye. There the harbours stretched out their quays to embrace the little boats, and pepper-pot lighthouses stood to shine them in. The strange shapes of the boards and fish-crates he painted on cast sudden light in Marian's mind on the curtains and window-frames that constricted the field of view in some of Stella's pictures. But the shape of memory was stranger still.

It dawned on her very clearly that it was to be near these, to be able to visit these, that Stella had settled near Cambridge. It had nothing to do with the flat, open land, or the old masters in the Fitzwilliam Museum.

At last she thought she had finished looking, but as she left she bought a little box of postcards, and as she opened the sample box to see what she got for the money there fell out of it facsimiles of Wallis's letters to Jim Ede, he who had made Kettle's Yard, and bought Wallis's pictures.

'*What I do mosely*,' she read in the clumsy laborious hand, '*is what use to be out of my own memery what we may never see again as things are altered altogether Ther is nothin whatever do not look like what it was . . .*'

Violet Garthen had said he painted like a child, Marian remembered. But the truth was he painted like an old man. With love, and with the ache of loss. She went back to his pictures again, and lingered till they closed the house at four. She had no doubt at all that if she had owned every single technically perfect work of Violet's she would have exchanged them all for a tiny piece of torn cardboard with a battered ship on it, riding a swelling wave. But she didn't have to – Stella had left her three of them. She was rich.

And now, back in the barn, she looked at Stella's pictures with a new eye. For all these furious landscapes and raging flowers, whether they were any good or not, were certainly full of Stella. They had in their way what Wallis had – expressive power. They were in the end, worthless or not, Stella's justification. Marian's own justification she told herself, as she had always done, was her children, and she felt the familiar little glow of superiority – surely it was better to have devoted oneself to flesh and blood, living and loving creatures, than to all this?

She prowled round the pictures all evening. She chose an open window, with a prospect of rooftops, chimney and sea for Violet, and paintings of themselves as children for Toby and Alice. And in the morning rang a removal and storage firm, and arranged to have them despatched to Cornwall, and the others all collected and stored until further notice. And then she rang the estate agent and told him he could clear the house and put it on the market at the weekend.

She needed to leave now. The disabled context, the sense of terminal disruption which inhabited the house made it desperately depressing. She called a taxi. And going into the barn she took Thomas Tremorvah from the easel. This picture was going with her — going, she realized, home. How to take a canvas in a taxi? She took the empty picture with the blue grounds, and tied them together face to face. And then at the last minute, suddenly appalled at the obliteration of all she would leave behind her, she seized Stella's ancient wooden paintbox, with its splattered surface and split lid, and lugged that away with her too.

It was early the following evening when the sequence of taxis and trains delivered Marian home again. With unwieldy things to carry, she struggled up the hill to the house in a light rain. She heard the sighing of a gentle surf on the beach below her as she climbed. Twice she stopped to look for the tiny transitory spark of the lighthouse in the dusk. She was tired when she got in. The pictures she put down in the hall, her case and Stella's paintbox she took upstairs to her room. She remembered the box in so many different places – poor battered old thing – she slipped the catches and opened it, and the ghostly smell of old turps took her by the throat. Somehow she had expected chaos and screwed up paint tubes in the box, but though nearly all the tubes were rolled up, partly used, they were in order, in rows beneath the palettes, both rubbed clean. When you pushed the box it slid backwards on its hinges, revealing a lower compartment, several inches deep, for bottles and brushes.

It contained besides these, a chunky brown paper parcel, somewhat stained. Marian lifted this out and turned it over. It said, 'Leo's money,' written in bold letters. She tore open one corner, and saw banknotes.

She was full of relief and joy. She seized it, and went tearing out again, almost laughing. She went directly to Leo's house, and rattled the door-knocker. When she got no answer she knocked again. A young woman looked out of an upstairs window next door.

'He's at the art class, I expect,' she said. 'He usually goes.'

'Where's that?'

'Back Street. Halfway along.' She closed her window.

Marian set out for Back Street. There was a luminous darkness, in which the sea contrived not to lose blueness, but to deepen it almost to vanishing point. The lighthouse shone like an intermittent evening star, bright windows round the harbour made gleaming watery banners hang in the sea. As she walked along the wharf she saw in the light of the street lamps to the sandy bottom of the harbour, the washerwoman wrinkled skin of the sand, the submerged ropes, even a tiny shoal of minuscule fishes visible in the scope of the sodium lamps.

She didn't know what she was looking for exactly, in

the intermittent light of the lamps, and the darkness under the stars. She stood hesitating in the street. As she stood there someone came past her, a white-haired woman in a red coat, who said, 'The art class? Upstairs.' Marian followed her up a flight of narrow wooden steps on the front of the house, and entered just behind her.

There were a lot of people in the room. Men and women. A rough circle of easels and chairs. It was a large room, open to the roof-beams, and very untidy. There was a sink in one corner, and work pinned up round the walls. Some rather good portraits were propped higgledy-piggledy in one corner. A low, very uncomfortable-looking couch was in the middle of the circle, covered with a scruffy blanket.

She saw Leo, partly hidden behind a huge easel right on the far side of the room, and went towards him.

He said, 'Here,' and thrust into her hands a dirty board, a sheet of paper, and a thick black crayon. 'There,' he said, indicating the only empty chair in the room.

'Leo, I just brought this . . .' she started.

Behind her two or three people were chatting to a young woman who stood barefoot beside the couch. Someone said, 'OK, Jo,' and she immediately took off what she was wearing – a short, coloured dressing-gown – and stood beside the teacher stark naked. He gestured, describing a pose. She sat down with one leg drawn up, and an arm resting on the knee. She was almost facing Marian. A skinny woman, with small breasts, and a large dark pubic bush. Long-limbed, face turned into the shadow cast by the lamp hanging on the beam above her. It was not that Marian had never seen a naked woman before; it was that she had never had – how could one have, except alone with a lover? – permission to stare. And that permission, of course, was conditional on an intention to draw. To have walked in off the street to stare, to see a naked stranger like a sideshow would have been intolerably squalid. And the woman was posed exactly between Marian and the door. To leave publicly would have been intolerably insulting.

'Fifteen minutes,' said the teacher. Marian sat down, took up a pencil and drew. And could not tell whether it was looking or drawing that was hard, but knew at once that this was harder than anything she had ever done.

At the end of the class Leo had looked at her desperate drawing, and nodded. 'That distance is too long compared with that one,' he said, 'so she looks too thin. I like that line—'

Marian said, 'I didn't mean to do this.'

'Why not?' he said. 'Half the people here are amateurs, and half are pros. It's not a discipline you grow out of. Come to the pub, and I'll introduce you to some people. Though I don't think there's anyone here tonight who would remember Stella.'

He had gathered his things, and put his coat on. She followed him into the street.

'I only meant to give you this,' she said, putting the packet into his hand.

'What is it?'

'What it says, I think. I haven't counted it.'

'It'll be right,' he said, looking at the scrawled label. 'That's a relief.'

'To both of us. I've been worried about all this.'

'You didn't have trouble getting the lawyer to release it?'

'The lawyer doesn't know about it. I found it, and brought it straight to you. And I won't come to the pub tonight, Leo. I've been travelling all day, and I'm tired.'

'Next week, then,' he said. 'Goodnight, Stella's daughter.'

'Ma,' said Toby, 'there's somebody I want you to meet.' Marian looked up from gardening. She had muddy gloves on her hands, and a pile of weeds lay on the ground in front of her. She had been working within the sound of the sea, and of the little rattling train going in and out of the station below. Digging herself in again, relishing her return. Lavender and fuchsia burgeoned along the terraced bed she was weeding, and Toby, standing on the level above her with his companion, was outlined against a dazzle of the descending afternoon light. So that it was only gradually, as she climbed the steps towards them, that she saw what it was about Matthew that was on Toby's mind.

'My Gran would like to see you, Mrs Easton,' the strange young man said. She was staring at him shamelessly. But you couldn't exactly stare at what was remarkable about him; the likeness to Toby was mercurial, glancing, something to do with movement, gesture, unconscious stance. Of course they were roughly of a height; their hair and eye colour, and the shape of nose and brow were like; but the startling thing depended on movement, and faded into a mere general similarity in stillness.

'I think *I'd* like to talk to *her*,' said Marian.

'This is Mathy, I should have said,' said Toby. 'Matthew Vanson. We'll take you to see his Gran any time you like.'

'As soon as I've washed my hands,' said Marian.

She washed them slowly, working at her fingernails with the nail-brush, shaken, gaining time. It hadn't occurred to her, though why ever not she couldn't now imagine, that her father might have connections other than herself. That he might have been a family man, with children and grandchildren who might resemble hers. She had imagined something perfectly simple, a young man going to his death no sooner than he had begotten her. A less dramatic truth was threatening. Had his disappearance simply been because he was married to someone else? All she wanted, she thought, was to know his name for sure; no, more, she wanted to know was he the man in the portrait?

She changed her shirt, and with clean hands went downstairs to where her son and his double waited for her.

Mathy's second Gran was in an old people's home. It was a large and rambling house in the upper part of the town. The inmates were sitting in a conservatory, lined up in easy chairs. It all glowed with light and warmth, and had a view of the neatened garden. A low buzz of conversation competed with the sound of the unwatched television set in the lounge behind it. But somehow the sense of displacement and diminishment was palpable.

The woman they had come to see was at the far end of the glassy room, half tucked away behind a huge pot plant. She looked very old, much older than Stella had looked, and her hands told her story at once. Arthritis had deformed them into the likeness of some exotic root vegetable. They lay in her lap, revealing helplessness. But they were not idle; a little square of knitting was in progress on a pair of red plastic needles gripped at a strange angle. She laid the work in her lap, looked up with a brightly alert expression, and said to Mathy, 'Well, let me 'ave a look, then.'

Mathy nudged Toby, who stood forward a fraction of a step, and said, 'Are you some kind of missing aunt of mine?'

'Don't know, my 'ansome,' she said. 'That's what we've got to work out. Some kind of great-auntie is what I might be. Then again you might be some sort of accidental looker. You two young cocks run along for a minute, while I talk to this lady here – Mrs Easton, id'n it?'

'Marian,' said Marian, sitting down in an empty cane chair facing her. 'And you are Mrs Tremorvah?'

'No, no. I'm a Poldavy, now. Mrs Betty Poldavy. But that's my marriage name. I was a Tremorvah. So if you be any kindred of mine, we be talking about something one of my brothers got up to, and never told about.'

'I'm sorry,' said Marian. 'I don't want to go round raking up old dirt.'

''Tis natural. You would want to know, though.'

'Yes.'

'And I have been racking my brains since Mathy told me. I have – I did have – four brothers. There was Steven, then Jamie. Both dead and gone now. But they was both married men in the war.'

'It's been known,' said Marian, quietly.

'Ess. Ess, it has. More than once. But I'd be surprised; very surprised. They was both very steady men. Family men. Chapel twice every Sunday. Then there was Peter;

he was a bit giddy, and he hadn't got settled when we lost him. His boat was run down in a fog off Gurnard's Head, and sank like a stone. Steven was with him. The boat that hit them got Steven out of the water, but Peter was gone.'

'When was that?' asked Marian.

'I can't hardly recollect. You're asking me to go back sixty years. Somewhere round about nineteen thirty-five.'

'It isn't him then. I'm too young.'

'Then there's only Thomas it can be. If it's any of them. Not just coincidental. Or some other branch of the family that carries on the likeness. Not that I know of anyone.'

'And if it was Thomas you would be my aunt,' said Marian.

'Ess, I would. But I never heard a breath of scandal about Thomas. Perhaps it would have been kept from me then; but I never heard of it later. Not as much as a shake of the head. Not about *that* kind of thing.'

About something else, Marian heard in her inflexion, maybe. But then perhaps these deeply devout people couldn't be told things? Perhaps there were a lot of secrets?

'My mother was a painter, Betty,' she said. 'Could a painter have been a friend of one of your brothers?'

'We didn't have much to do with the artists,' she said. 'It was perfectly friendly. They went their ways, we went ours. They were a good thing for the town, when the fishing went down. They would pay for old sheds and sail-lofts, and they needed rooms. They were a Godless lot, mind. Not a chapel-goer among them, and precious few church-goers.'

'Would St Ives people have been willing to sit as models for the artists?' Marian asked.

'Oh, ess. There were portraits made, by artists and photographers. Lots of portraits. I remember earning a shilling from Mrs Walsh to sit still while she drawed me as a girl. A whole shilling. You should look in the Sloop Inn. I'm told that's full of drawings of local people. You should look there.'

Marian felt stymied. Could she, should she say, 'My mother painted your brother Thomas stark naked – how did that come about?' The taboo about not bad-mouthing the dead is powerful.

But Mrs Poldavy hadn't fallen silent, just thoughtful. 'I recall Tommy being very hot to join the navy,' she said. 'Father didn't want to have him go, but he wouldn't stop.'

'Didn't he have to go?'

'Not have to, no. Fishing was what they called a reserve occupation. He volunteered. He couldn't wait to get out of the town, I heard Jamie say. It left them short-handed in the boat they worked. But there it was. He would go off, and he never came back.'

'And it wasn't a scandal that drove him out?'

'Not the kind you're thinking about, no.'

'So why did he leave, do you think?'

'I couldn't tell you. You'd have to ask him.'

'Ask him?' cried Marian, nearly jumping out of her chair. 'But I thought he was dead!'

'He idn't dead,' said Mrs Poldavy. 'He's over to Gwithian.'

Alice sat in the bay window of the flat, with the sweep of the bay shining at her round a hundred and eighty degrees. It was a brisk sort of day, with little flickering white horses breaking all over the sea. A big cloud, pearly primrose above and dirty black below, stood over the Island behind the town, seeming to be anchored there by a band of rainbow. The lighthouse had retreated into sheets of rain, and only one person was walking on the sands below. Alice had brought herself a cup of coffee, and *The Times* to read on the window-seat. She flicked through the paper, desultory, only half able to take her eyes from the view. But the concert advertisement leapt off the page at her – her quartet, playing Mozart and Shostakovitch at the Wigmore Hall. They must be rehearsing without her – worse – the advertisement gave the names of the quartet players, and the violist was someone else. Without telling or warning her, Max had replaced her.

She had not even the consolation of anger, not for more than a few minutes. For of course she had left a rehearsal to go to her grandmother's bedside. You make choices, and you live with them. How if she had stayed put, and sent a message? She imagined it – Toby leaning over Stella's immobile form, and saying, 'Gran, Alice can't come, she has a rehearsal.' She saw at once that her mother would have been outraged, deeply hurt, and that Stella, assuming the message had got through to her, would have perfectly understood. Stella would have expected it of her to the point where, in coming to her grandmother's death scene, she had ignored her grandmother's example.

So why had she done it? Out of love, of course. It was what she had urgently wanted to do. She had adored and admired her grandmother. But the problem in life, she saw now, was not so much doing what you wanted, as doing what you wanted *most*.

The road to Gwithian winds right round the bay. Marian drove it alone; she didn't know why she hadn't told Toby and Mathy, hadn't told Alice, hadn't told Leo when he came to supper, what had emerged. She didn't know what she was opening – happiness or calamity. How could she know when she didn't know why Stella had kept this secret?

Through dismal suburban-seeming Carbis Bay, and pretty Lelant, then across the causeway road at the back of the Saltings – the tide was out as she went, and the birds were flocking and feeding. Then Hayle, with its derelict engineering works, where once the best steam engines in the world had been made, Leo had told her, and now timber yards squatted in the ruination. But there were some working boats in the pool. And then Copperhouses, straggling out along the waterside, along the Gwithian road. The whole landscape here was strange with blown sand. Mountains of sand were wind-piled on this side of the bay, grassed over, making knobbly lumpy hillocks, high as hills, high enough to conceal the sea entirely from the little road, stretching deep enough inland to have side-roads labelled for campsites, to have a huge derelict works of some description in the midst of them. On the right of the road, the inland side, the peaceful farmland rolled gently away eastwards, quite unconcerned, as though the sea were nowhere near, and nothing was engulfed and buried by the dunes.

Gwithian was a pretty place; a small village with a church, a chapel, some thatched cottages, and a wildly discordant Edwardian brick pub. No shop; or not one Marian could find. She parked the car beside the pub, and went in to ask.

'Mr Tremorvah?' said the barman. 'Sorry, don't know 'im.'

But the barmaid, appearing with a tray of clean glasses, said, 'We got a Captain Tremorvah. That who you mean?'

'Who's he, then, jinks?' the barman asked.

'Doddery old geezer. Used to drink here when he first came, but the Methodees has got him now,' the girl said. 'Not in the village. He's over on the Towans. Go back to Hayle a bit and turn right.'

The road wound improbably among the tussocks, sand showing through bent-grass meadows on either side. It seemed as though it could only possibly be a track to the beach. But it led first to a spectacular prospect of the sea, rolling under a rain-laden, sullen sky, and then to a startling view of Godrevy Island, Godrevy lighthouse, standing up stark and near, stripped of the charms of distance. The white tower was octagonal, the round garden at its foot was dark green with clumps of gorse, it stood grimly admonitory on a rough pyramid of black jagged rock fretted over by breaking water. The road petered out in a colony of ramshackle buildings – shacks and bungalows and wooden houses standing in squares of picket-fenced sandy garden, several deep along unmade roads. Every one was different – there were one or two quite well-made houses, clapboarded, painted. Most were small and evoked that pungent pathos of half-time places, boarded-up places, places down on their luck, places that prosper at some other time of year. There was a shop – a beach-booth sort of shop, and a phone box. Marian asked for directions, and got sent further on.

It was almost the last house. A little white bungalow with a corrugated iron roof, a glazed porch facing the sea, a new stainless steel stove-pipe chimney, a flagpole in the garden, sharing the space with two palm trees and a clump of pampas grass. It was perched rather high on a tussock, and in front of it the whole bay spread out in view. Marian rang the bell – a hanging ship's bell with a knotted rope to clang it with. She waited, and rang again, and waited again. A smart wind blew off the immense beach behind her. The waves rolled onto it, breaking twenty deep, making, there were so many, not the soft rhythmical sounds of the beaches back there, but an uninterrupted steady blurred loud roaring. She rang again, and had turned to go when the inner door was opened, and an old man came towards her across the porch.

He had an upright bearing, but he moved unsteadily. His hair was white, but still stood up in a thick shock from his forehead. He stared at Marian through the glass, and then slowly, with visible reluctance, opened the door. 'Yes?' he said.

Marian said, 'I think you may be my father.'

Time had leached all the colour out of him. He stood at his door wearing a sandy-coloured sweater, a faded and pallid man, his dark eyes the only vivid thing about him. 'No,' he said. 'You have been misinformed.'

Marian stood there, disconcerted. Didn't her blue eyes come from her father? Stella's eyes were dark, like this old man's.

'I am Stella Harnaker's daughter,' she said, and she saw him react. Some minute, quickly repressed gleam in his eyes. He knew that name.

'I have no children,' he said.

'But you remember my mother?'

'I know her name. You should ask her—'

'She's dead now.'

He had begun to back away, holding the door as if to close it on Marian. He stopped. A silence lengthened between them.

'Please,' she said, 'please . . .'

He stood back for her to enter the porch, and they stood between the plastic chairs facing out across the shore. He closed the door, and the clamorous surf was muted. A fly buzzed, helpless against the glass. It fell to the sill, and at once rose and tried again.

'What do you want?' he said.

She was shaken with anger. She was outraged by his impassiveness, by this cruel lying. Then she suddenly realized that he was trembling slightly, holding tightly onto the back of the flimsy chair, saying, 'What do you want?' His eyes were watery, clouded. She could not tell if it was grief, or shock, or just old age that confronted her.

'Tell me,' she said.

'I don't know you,' he said. 'You have been misinformed.'

'You do know,' she said. 'You must remember! Don't you remember wading in to save me, holding me all night buttoned in your coat at Kynance? Tell me about it . . .'

'I have never been to Kynance in my life,' he said. 'I have never been there.'

She caught again his glance askance from hers. He was lying. Why should he lie?

'Go away,' he said. 'Leave me alone.'

'I will go,' she said. 'But – I haven't got the wrong person entirely, have I? You are Thomas Tremorvah – you are the man who missed the boat?'

'You know about that then,' he said.

'A little. It's all forgotten, now.'

'Oh, no. No, it isn't.' There was barely a trace of Cornish in his voice. He sounded like what he was – a retired naval officer. He could have come from anywhere.

'It's so long ago,' said Marian. She stepped out of the door, into the bluff pressure of the wind, cold now, and bringing a spittle of rain on its breath. The darkness of the sky had settled down on the water, and blanked out the opposite shore entirely.

'You go and ask them over there if they have forgotten,' the old man said, 'You go and ask.'

And he closed the door.

She started by asking about the lifeboat disaster in the fish shop in Downalong. Over bright mackerel and pearly scallops they told her there were people who could still remember it. They'd be getting on a bit, now. It had all been in the hands of God, the fishmonger added.

'Why did God save one man and let the others perish?' Marian wondered aloud.

With fervent emphasis, the men behind the counter told her. Margaret Freeman was a good woman, a woman who had raised three generations of her family. God had saved William Freeman because his wife needed him. It was clear to them, and they seemed to have not a shadow of uncertainty in their faith. As for anyone having heard voices, they added, angels telling him what to do, they didn't know about that . . .

'There's a lot that's never been told yet,' said a customer, overhearing. 'William Freeman seen a band of bright light showing him the way to climb the cliff to safety. A shining light to guide him.'

'Where would I find someone who could tell me about it?' Marian asked.

'Try asking in the lodges on the quay,' the fishmonger said. 'Someone 'ull remember.'

The lodges were three shacks on the harbour waterside.

Marian had wandered past them, and seen the notice, declaring that strangers might sit in the open shelter between them only by invitation. She hesitated. 'Am I – is a woman – allowed to call in there?'

'You'll find lots of old fogeys in there,' they told her, 'but you can go in. They've got history; photographs and things.'

Marian knocked before going in. It was a large square wooden cabin. In the middle of the floor a little stove and chimney pipe gave out heat. The old men were sitting on benches, lined up around the walls. Most of them sat with their backs to the window towards the harbour. There was a handsome old clock, and a barometer. A rather good painting of the harbour beach hung at the back, and otherwise the walls were entirely covered with old photographs.

'May I come in?' Marian said. 'I was told you could tell me about the lifeboat; the one that was lost before the war.'

One of the old men got to his feet. He led her across the room, and pointed to a photograph. It showed her a lifeboat of a shape familiar from the collecting boxes, open amidships, with a small canopy back and front. It was on a trolley, and a crew were lined up in lifejackets, standing in front of it. But it did not seem to interest the old man much. He began to point out to her one by one the old pictures of the town – here the back of the beach when the seine boats were pulled up under the railway arches; here the station buildings before they were demolished for a car-park; here the rocky point tipped by a mining tower, where now a hotel stands . . . mixed in with the old topography were numerous shipwrecks, going back years and years, to the days of sail. He named the vessels, and their dates, as though he were reading tombstones. Around her the other men resumed a desultory conversation. But they were all watching her.

Marian's eye was caught by a boat burning – on fire on the rocks, swathed in flames with the surf breaking just beyond. 'What's that?' she asked her guide.

'That's the boat you were asking after,' he said.

'On fire?' Nobody had mentioned fire to her yet.

'We burn a boat if there's been loss of life in her,' he told her. 'Tradition.'

'Do you remember it?' she asked him.

'Ess. Yes.'

'Were you there?'

'No. I was tucked up in bed with my brother.'

'But you remember it?'

'Afterwards. I remember the morning afterwards. We all do.'

'Could anybody tell me about that? About what it was like?'

She waited while they thought about it.

'She ought to talk to Margaret Freeman,' someone said.

'Freeman?' said Marian. 'William Freeman's daughter?'

'His widow,' they told her.

They seemed somehow to have decided something, wordlessly. Marian's guide said, 'There's cousins of hers here. By marriage, that is. We'll ask her. We'll see if she'll talk to you. You come by tomorrow, and we'll let you know. All right?'

'Thank you,' said Marian.

Her guide took the two steps to show her to the door. His untaught, princely courtesy abashed her. He was on his own ground absolutely, and she had been an honoured guest. She could find no words to let him know she had understood that.

Mrs Freeman had agreed to be called on. Marian found her sitting in the front room of a house just one row behind the great beach, within sound of the sea. She was tucked in an armchair beside the fire, working a needlepoint picture of the Good Shepherd. Her feet were in slippers, and she looked frail, but she had that bright alertness that shines in some people in old age. A quiet lady, Marian thought; a shrewd lady. The room was full of photographs and flowers – her four generations in every age of childhood and adult life smiled out of photo frames. Someone in naval uniform, someone in graduate's robes, holding a scroll . . .

'What do you want to know?' Mrs Freeman asked her.

I want to understand, thought Marian, but what can I ask? 'Was your husband in the regular crew of the lifeboat?' she asked.

'No,' Mrs Freeman told her. 'He was in the rowing lifeboat that preceded the motor lifeboats, but he had never set foot in that boat before.'

'But it was short-crewed? The cox needed volunteers?'

The two who didn't hear the maroons had been rehoused in the council houses further up the town, Mrs Freeman told her. 'They didn't hear the rockets. And *I* believe them; my brother who also lived up there didn't hear them.'

'Tell me how it happened that your William went with the boat . . .'

Mrs Freeman began to talk, softly and fluently.

'We lived in Victoria Place, then, just behind the harbour. We had a child sick, Susan, she was nine then, seriously ill. We were up nights and nights with her. She was just fallen asleep that night, and we were going to our bed. William went up to the top window to look out at the storm. "William you aren't going nowhere," I said. "Come to bed," I said. He was just getting into bed, he had one leg out of his trousers, when the maroon went up. There was the sound of men running in the street outside the door. William put his trousers back on, and went out. I went to the door, looking out. I followed William down to the wharf. And someone comes up with his lifejacket in his hand, and said, "I can't go, boy." '

'Was it someone you knew?' Marian asked.

'Oh ess, I knew him. He was married to a cousin of mine. So William took the jacket. That's stale news. And my brother was down there on the slip. I was saying to William, "Think what you've got at home." I suppose I was whimpering, really, and my brother said, "Goest home, Margaret, she's as safe as houses." And that was the last word he said to me. He was gone, then.'

'With that I took William's cap, and gave him the tam-o'-shanter I was wearing. I was stood outside the Sloop, and the women were at Chy an Chy, at the top of the slipway. William's mother was there, and she cried out, "William, you ain't going!" '

'Matthew Barber said to me, "Take her in, take her in." '

'That was fifty-six years ago; he had a niece born on the same day.

'I went back in to my daughter. Night went on – he oughter bin back. I put his dry clothes to warm by the fire. Men going up and down, running from door to door – nobody came in to tell me anything. I remember I knelt down to a chair in my kitchen, and I said, "Lord, you know where they are . . ."

'I went out just coming light on the twenty-third – those January nights it's pitch black outside. So I could see a bit of daylight coming in, I'd move the curtains now and then, have a peep out to see. I thought I'll go down the wharf again now – children were quiet, and I think Susan had gone asleep and I met a neighbour as I was going along the road, she said, "Oh, it's awful, Margaret, idn' it?"

'I said, "The weather is dreadful."

'She said, "I mean the lifeboat."

'I said, "What's the matter with the lifeboat? My man's on it." And she looked horrified at me, I never saw her disappear, she just completely vanished from me – she went like the wind.

'Well, what with that, I started to cry then. I went home to my mother. She never knew anything about it, father had been out, he hadn't come back. I just blurted out to my poor mother that the lifeboat had gone, so mother went screaming out as well by the back door, I can see her now, poor soul – John was in, you see, her eldest boy – and she knew Willy had gone too, because she was down on the wharf as well when the lifeboat went, she was down crying, you see, "Oh you aren't going, you shan't go," and all that sort of thing.

'So as we went out together there's others running up. "Your man's all right, Margaret. He be all right – he be over to Gwithian."

'I said, "*My man's* all right? How do be the others?"'

There was silence then. Two women in the room, strangers to each other, thinking about the dead.

'What had happened to William?' Marian asked.

He had told her afterwards. The first time the boat turned over, the cox, and William Barber and Edgar Basset and John Thomas were thrown out. The engine stalled. There were four left. Dick went forward to start the motor, and Dick was thrown out as she went over again. Then there were three of them in under the canopy. William had said, "Hold on boys – where she's agoing, I'm agoing with her," – he wedged his hand someway under the canopy.

'She was already in the shore surf, when Jack and Matthew were thrown out – William couldn't think how, Jack was wedged behind him in the canopy, he felt him flying over his head. They were so close in, William thought had there been anybody there, they would have been saved. Over and over he asked himself, "How come they two didn't hang on, just that minute!"

'She landed flat on a rock, and William walked out over. He thought he should have been washed away, still with his boots and lifejacket on. But he climbed out of the reach of the waves. He thought he would die of cold, just sat there. So he took off his sea-boots that were full of water, and climbed the cliff in his stockinged feet. He'd never been to Gwithian before, and didn't know where he was. He went first to a chalet, where he had no reply, and then walked on and fell over a hedge into the lane leading to a farmhouse.

'He knocked on the door, and the farmer put his head out of the window, and said, "What is it, what do you want?"

'William said, "I'm now washed in on the lifeboat."

'The farmer could see his lifejacket. They were as good as gold. They brought him in and stripped him and gave him dry clothing, the farmer's wife dressing – "I can see her now in her corsets!" William used to say – and they came out of their warm bed and put William in it. He could see through the window the lights bobbing and bobbing along the shore, and he knew they were looking for him.

'The first person to reach the farmhouse was William's cousin. William was not coherent; they thought he was, but he wasn't. He was telling them to go get Matthew and Jack from the rocks.

'The farmer's wife kept him the day, and he was brought home to me in the evening.'

'What did you say to him?' Marian asked.

'What could I say? I didn't hardly know him.'

'Your husband was a brave man, Mrs Freeman.'

'He wouldn't have liked you to say that. He wouldn't have it called brave.'

'I was told he saw a band of light, guiding him up the cliffs.'

'You've been listening to a bit of romancing, there.'

'And afterwards – was there ill feeling?'

'There were twenty-one widows and orphans left in the town,' Mrs Freeman told her. 'Mrs Cocking lost her husband, her son and her son-in-law in the one night. I wouldn't want to tell you about it. That man who gave his jacket to William saying that he heard like a whisper telling him he shouldn't go. People saying they were only after medals, they all had medals, they was after more . . . I wouldn't like to tell you about all that.'

'Was William angry about it? Did he resent the men who missed the boat?'

'My husband was one as didn't show his feelings,' she said.

'What happened about your little girl? The one who was sick?' Marian asked.

'She died. Not then. She got better then. But she died at thirty-three, of breast cancer. Just like her father, never mentioned it. Left it too late. She left four children for me to bring up.'

They began to look together at photographs of those children, and their children, and the certificate of honour – the bronze medal citation given to William Freeman by the Lifeboat Institution, and hanging in the hall. Marian took her leave. And Mrs Freeman resumed stitching the woolly fleece of one of the flock at the feet of the Good Shepherd.

Marian walked up to the top of the Island, in a bright patch of day, and looked across to the green headland, and the cheerful distant lighthouse, forefending shipwreck. If you had sharp eyes and you knew they were there you could just make out the specks of white and ochre that were the huts and chalets on Gwithian Towans. And Thomas Tremorvah had been right; none of this was yet forgotten. It was as raw as yesterday.

And it was a hero tale. Everyone had helped her hear this – but what she needed was the other story, the shadow story, the one about someone who didn't go, who missed the boat. It was natural enough, they didn't want to talk about that. She would have to ask Leo to help her.

Marian knocked on Leo's door, and stood waiting. He opened up to her in stockinged feet, holding his shoes in his hand.

'Alice is here,' he said, as though she might have known that, and come looking.

'It was you I wanted,' she said.

'Come in,' he said. He looked more than usually dishevelled. He led her down the stairs, and into his work-shop. There was no sign of Alice.

Marian noticed at once the grades of order, shading into confusion in the large room. At the far end of the room a dirty canvas sheet covered something standing in the ruins of a dismantled packing case.

'Your mother's here,' said Leo to the apparently empty room.

Alice came quietly up behind Marian, and stood beside her, barefoot, and put an arm round her mother's waist.

'Hullo, love,' said Marian. 'I didn't expect to find you here.'

'So what did you want then, Marian?' said Leo. They were all talking without looking at each other.

'Some help, Leo. That man who got out of the boat, on the night of the disaster – the man who wouldn't go—'

'He didn't have a regular jacket,' said Leo. 'He wasn't regular crew. He didn't have to go. He volunteered in the first place, and then he changed his mind. You could say he was right, really, but he wasn't easily forgiven. He's dead now.'

'Who would remember him? Who could and would tell me about him, do you know?'

'It isn't him you're looking for,' said Leo.

'I know,' said Marian. 'But he's part of the picture. I'm trying to get the picture.'

'Leave it with me,' said Leo. 'I'll see what I can do.'

Squashed round a black table in the Sloop, Toby and Mathy, and Mathy's sister Ann, were drinking together.

'There's a sort of compensation built in,' Mathy told Toby. 'Scarcer the fish get, the better the price you get. The old men say it's all finished, and it has gone down almost to nothing compared to what they remember, when there was seven hundred fishermen in St Ives. And it will be worse when the Spanish get here, next year.'

'But you're managing?'

'I wish. It's not a bad life; you 'aven't got an employer on your back. No bosses, only the tides. There idn't anything I'd rather do.'

'So what's the problem with going on with it?' Toby asked.

'The boat's the problem. That *Mary Ann* we was out on just now be all wormeaten. There's more caulk than tar in her bottom. Had her days. My uncle worked her, and my great-uncle worked her, and I've got the use of her because she idn't worth selling on. But you could do all right with the right boat.'

'What sort of boat would that be?'

'A new one would be the thing. Eighteen footer, right for the harbour here. And set up for pleasure trips, and line fishing. The tourists like fishing. You could take fishing trips in summer, and fish on your own account in winter. And not hardly go out in rough weather.'

'What would a boat like that cost?' asked Toby. He kept catching Ann's eye. She was very quiet, but she was watching him.

'Thousands that I 'aven't got,' said Mathy. 'For a good boat and a licence. You need a licence to land fish. And the banks won't lend for boats any more. There isn't the sort of money in it that they like to see. So that's that. One more season out of the old boat and I'll be grounded.'

'Mathy will be all right,' said Ann, suddenly. 'His girl-friend has a nice little business doing gateaux and all that for the hotels. It isn't so hard for women,' she added. 'We've been doing bed and breakfast and working in hotels since anyone can remember. Hasn't changed so much for us.'

'Well, I'm off,' said Matthew, putting his empty beer glass down on the table. 'Got to get Rachel fetched up to the Tregenna for the disco tonight.'

'Are you going to the disco, Ann?' said Toby, seeing his chance.

'No,' she said. 'Not so far.'

'Well, are you allowed to go dancing with someone born eastwards of Hayle Bar?'

Ann laughed. 'I was hoping you might ask that,' she said.

Marian was lying on her bed. The moon was framing itself neatly in the upper left hand pane of her window, and she had not closed it out with her curtains, so only the moon could see her, lying on her front, head propped up, looking at her life-drawings. She had moved the bedside lamp so that it illuminated them brightly. They were not as bad as she had feared they would be; her first attempt was the worst, but not perhaps because it was the most totally unpractised, but because after the first shock, she had thought the young woman beautiful, as indeed, she realized now, the most unremarkable human body in fact is; the result had been a fuzzy drawing.

Her shot at the second pose had been better. It had been a ten-minute pose, and haste had made her simplify. The teacher had called for shorter and shorter poses, down to one minute, and Marian had been driven into ferocious concentration, and airier and airier results. Then there had been another, longer pose. Refocussed, Marian had stared with an ice-cold vision. An almost cruel accuracy of view. The girl on the couch was cradling her head in her arms, and her knees were drawn up to her belly. And you needed to see, not what you knew about arms and hands and feet, about human bulk, about the comfort or discomfort of the posture the girl was in; you needed simply to see what curve exactly the pressure on the muscles made the arm adopt, exactly where the thumb on the interlaced fingers emerged into view beside the nose, exactly how the upturned foot was seen beside the calf of the other leg. The sole of the foot was filthy from the dusty floorboards, and the dirt defined the instep and the complex valley between the ball of the foot and the toes . . .

There had been a coffee break. She had at once turned to Leo, and told him she had something for him. 'Not now,' he said. 'Come for a drink later.' He had been looking very intently at the work on his easel, and while she wondered whether to escape – but the truth is she had partly wanted to stay – the session resumed. Marian had been drawing a slender and attenuated person, with a very small head. She struggled to make her drawings proportional. Looking at them now she saw no merit in them, except as rehearsals for another try. She saw that they were attempts at a certain kind of thing – the drawing made of shadowless outline. Absolutely simple. The moulding would be implicit in the line. At the coffee break she had contrived to get glimpses of what the others were working on, and seen how most of them were using sweeps of medium, paint or pastels, to make shadow and highlight do the work she was loading onto pure line. But it had seemed to be not the form to go around openly looking at other people's work. There was a murmur of conversation; two girls were talking to the model about some surfing incident that afternoon on the beach.

And Marian had felt completely at home in this coffee break, though lost in the art and craft entirely. Some of the people in the room knew each other, some did not. They were distantly friendly, but detached, their pre-occupation was with what was pinned on their easels. They were islanded, each marooned on the difficult shores of art. They probably each knew where they were, but not where the others were, or what signal from this deep solitude would reach a passing ship. It felt, in fact, like the rehearsal intervals in Alice's concerts. How many hundred such occasions had Marian sat through, when Alice was little, reading a book? The musicians were engulfed in music and the chat was deceitful, it was to pretend mini-mally that other people existed in a room where the masterpiece being worked on was alone.

Oddly, the best of Marian's drawings, she thought now, was one of the most rapidly made – a five-minute pose. And however minimal the merits of this piece of work, it had defined the task for her. The nature of the task was to discern the exact position of the intersection between a physical object and the light, and draw a line round it. She had always supposed, in all those years as Stella's daughter, that the difficulty – an insuperable difficulty for anyone but the most crazed devotee – was in the drawing, or the painting, come to that; that the difficulty was technical. A mere two hours trying it had taught her that what came first was seeing. The model's nakedness had dazzled her like the rising sun. She had had to struggle not to avert her eyes, to look steadily at the pensive face, the soft breast, the complex magenta cavity in the pubic hair, to look unflinching, until she saw enough to move the pencil on the paper. What was hard was to see the shape of another person, uncovered whole, as an absolute in the light, like a bare rock in the tides of the shore. She struggled to keep her feet in waves of misplaced emotion, feeling and rejecting embarrassment, admiration, jealousy, repulsion, curiosity – curiosity most of all – before arriving at something cool and hard: simple attention.

'Could one – could anyone – ' Marian wondered, 'look at themselves like that? Could I look at myself like that? And what would I see if I did?'

In the depths of the night something woke her. One of the children awake, moving in the darkened house. She got up at once, as she had always done, ready to comfort the bad dream, make the hot chocolate, take the temperature, find the aspirin . . . or slip quietly away if nothing was wrong. The habit of motherhood could not be thrown off. She stood on the landing, listening. And just as the stillness would have sent her back to bed she heard a soft clunk, clunk below her, somewhere downstairs. She put on slippers and went down. Cool air flowed in the hallway – the front door was ajar. Blown open? Hardly – but it was knocking gently to and fro. It had been latched open, so that it could not close and lock itself against someone . . . someone had gone out. She looked at her watch. One o'clock.

She went rapidly upstairs to Alice's room – she knew it would be Alice. Alice's bed was empty, rumpled. Her clothes were tumbled on the bedside chair. Her viola case was open on the pillow, likewise empty. Marian ran downstairs again, and grabbed her coat from the row of hooks by the door, putting it on over her nightdress. Alice's coat was still there.

Once outside she did not know which way to turn. Along the road seemed unlikely, so she plunged into the double darkness of the trees and bushes which overarched the cliff path. Her own natural direction would have been towards the beach, but as her eyes got used to darkness – it was not true darkness, there was moonlight – she could see the expanse of sand below her, faintly illuminated with nobody on it. So she went the other way. She did not call her daughter; she was afraid instinctively that a revealed pursuit might precipitate – what?

She had not talked to Alice about Leo, she was too appalled for that. Max was bad enough – but someone as old as Leo? A flip psychological reasoning occurred to her – Alice had grown up without men. Long lost grandfather, absconding father, other grandparents far off in California – no, such reasons cheapened Alice – Marian hurried on.

She slipped and stumbled on the rough footing – the soles of her slippers did not buffer the edges of the broken stones underfoot – brambles snagged her nightdress hem unseen. Then the path opened out. A bridge over the railway line led out onto a rocky promontory. There were no tall bushes there – only heather and bracken in the clefts between massive boulders, and a muted vision of the bay in moonlight opened before her. Overhead the stars were thick – visible in their millions, blurred into streamers of cloudy brightness like sequinned scarves of light. Faintly, from somewhere beyond her, Marian heard music.

Alice was standing on the edge of the drop to the sea, her nightdress billowing in the cool air, playing. Marian found her quickly, drawn by the heartbreaking sound. For the viola part was terrible, if heard alone. Mutilated, meaningless, like something fierce and caged. The violins and the cello gave the music warmth, melody, meaning. Just now and then the melody was passed to the viola, and Alice played the singing line, disembodied, eerily soaring – for the drive and depth had passed over to the other, unheard instruments – like flowing water out of rough rock. And then the grinding urgency resumed.

Marian listened, desolate, to Alice's naked unself-sufficiency revealed, while below her the great slow metronome of the bay – the rhythmic breaking waves, the winking lighthouse – marked time in the darkness.

Marian shivered – Alice must be bone-frozen in the cool air – and she hesitated. Somewhere in her mind she feared that disturbing Alice might make her fall – it would be to her death if she did.

And then someone came running noisily, Toby, leaping on the rocks, passing Marian and shouting, 'Alice *you silly cow!* What the hell are you doing? Come here! Come in!'

Marian shut her eyes, but Alice did not fall. Toby reached her, stooped, swept one arm round her shoulders and the other behind her knees, and caught her up in his arms. He carried her back from the brink, and set her down beside his mother.

'What *is* going on?' he said. 'It's the middle of the bloody night!'

'I didn't want to wake you,' Alice said.

'So why not wait till morning? Come on in, before one of us gets pneumonia.'

The moon was setting behind them, and a cold wind blew at their backs.

They put Alice to bed with a hot-water bottle, and a mug of hot milk and whisky. She was silent and passive, as obedient as a little child.

'Is she going mad, Mother, do you think?' asked Toby

quietly, when Alice's door was safely closed. 'Look, get some sleep if you can. She should be all right till morning – I've confiscated her bow.'

And then the quiet remainder of the night was followed by a quiet day. Alice sat silent, barely acknowledging the concern of her mother and brother, the offers of a walk, a coffee, the loan of a detective novel. They retreated, drawing an invisible line round her, leaving her in peace. She did not ask for the return of her bow, and the house was silent. She slept some of the afternoon – well she must need to – and when she got up she said, 'I'm going to see Leo,' and went out.

'So this is to do with Leo,' said Toby, grimly. 'Shall I go and knock his teeth in?'

'Counterproductive, I should think,' said Marian. 'Oh, God, I can't talk now, Toby. I'm taking the Garthen woman out to dinner.'

'Where are we going?' said Violet, putting her coat on.

'The Pig'n'Fish' said Marian. 'I booked a table for eight o'clock. There's lots of time.'

'I put that out for you to look at,' said Violet, indicating a black photograph album on the coffee table.

Marian sat down to look at it, feeling uncomfortable, with Violet standing, coat on, in the door, ready to go.

But as soon as she opened the album she was gripped. Young Stella stood in a garden somewhere, holding baby Marian. She had been a handsome woman, then, black-haired, straight and tall, wearing an elegant, simple dark dress. Violet stood beside and a little behind her, recognizably Violet, pretty and a little unkempt. Then a group of people in fancy dress, on a rigged up stage—

'That was *Measure for Measure* at the Arts Club,' said Violet, who had come to stand behind Marian's chair, looking over her shoulder. 'And that' – Marian had turned the page – 'was a civil defence exercise – home volunteers, it was called – we were supposed to be trained fire-fighters.'

A blurred and tiny photograph showed a group of men and women wearing tin hats and holding an enormous hose. They seemed to be practising in Tregenna Place.

Marian turned the thick black page. A park somewhere, with palm trees, and the top of the St Ives church tower in view. Tiny Marian was in that picture, too. She was running away from the camera, hands held up, towards Stella who was leaning down, arms outstretched, towards her. Stella was smiling, and the expression on her face was of unequivocal, radiant love.

'Have any of these that you want,' said Violet. 'I never look at them now.'

'I'd like this one very much,' Marian said. 'I don't remember—'

'You were too young to remember,' said Violet. There was a strange timbre in her voice, and Marian did not complete her sentence. She turned another page.

Now she was looking at Violet with a young soldier. He had an arm round Violet's shoulder, and they faced the camera and smiled guilelessly. Violet was wearing a bright print dress, covered with pansies. Marian knew they were pansies, knew the purple and yellow and blue colours of the print; it leapt out at her from the faded sepia photograph and took her breath away.

'That's my Bob,' said Violet. 'We were engaged to be married. But he was killed on manoeuvres. They didn't even get him to the battlefront – they just killed him on an exercise at Slapton Sands. Have you ever heard of Slapton Sands? No, well . . . I never got over it, in a way, though I was happy enough married to Malcolm while it lasted. You wouldn't remember Bob, of course.'

'I remember the dress,' said Marian.

'Hadn't we better be going?' said Violet. 'You can borrow the album if you like. Look at it at home.'

Marian possessed herself while they walked slowly, at Violet's pace, down the hill, in a deepening dusk. A pink sunset reflected off a bank of clouds in the east, towards Carn Brea, shone in delicate pearly iridescence on a calm sea. But soon they were lower down in the town, where they could not see over the rooftops. The Pig'n'Fish had only a glancing narrow view of sea past the car-park of the waterfront pub, and the two women faced each other without the distractions of the scene outside.

'I'm told my mother's best time was when she was here,' said Marian when they had ordered their food and wine. 'Why did she leave, Violet?'

'I don't know, I don't know. We weren't close any more, by that time. It had something to do with the way you were turning out, I think, but I didn't understand it.'

'This photograph,' Marian opened the album on the table. 'I remember that dress. It was your dress . . .' Her intonation was balanced between statement and query.

'Yes. I loved those great blowsy thirties prints. Of course, everything suits you when you're young.'

'You never lent it to Stella?'

'God, no. She wouldn't have been seen dead in it!'

'So it wasn't Stella. It was you.'

'What was me?'

'You that took me to Kynance.'

'So you do remember. I was afraid you might.'

'Not properly,' said Marian. 'Tell me about it.'

She saw to her surprise that Violet was struggling with some strong emotion. But she couldn't have expected the remark, from a grown woman, with which Violet replied, almost wailing, 'It wasn't my fault. You were palmed off on me. I did my best . . .'

'Tell me properly,' said Marian quietly, 'as though I couldn't remember anything.'

'I promised I would look after you while Stella went up to London. She had an offer from a big gallery there to give her an exhibition. It was very difficult in the war; but she had this chance, and she wanted to take some pictures and go. So I said I'd look after you. Then the night before she was due back, he rang up, wanting to see you—'

'Who rang up?'

'A man who said he was your father. I didn't know who he was from Adam, Stella hadn't let on about it. It was still a terrible disgrace in those days. Of course there were lots of young men killed in the war, it wasn't unusual to have a young widow with a child. But Stella wouldn't fib about it; she just brazened it out and gave you her own name. He asked for Stella, of course, but also for you. His ship was in the Carrack Roads – that's off Falmouth. He had a ticket of leave, but only for twelve hours. Someone from the ship was going to the radio station on the Lizard, he could get that far. So I borrowed a car and took you to meet him. We went down to the cove at Kynance . . . Then you wandered off, and the tide came in . . .'

'I remember that bit,' said Marian.

'Tommy got to you in time, but he couldn't get back. I panicked. I phoned the Falmouth harbour–master to get through to the ship, to tell them what had happened, and I phoned Stella. I rang and rang her until she got in, and her train was very late, and she got the police to drive her over. She was very angry. We waited for you all night. We lit a fire on the cliff-top, and some of the ship's officers came over, and they used a lamp to Morse code to him. We could see him in the moonlight, but he hadn't got a torch to answer the messages. I was petrified. I didn't know what had happened to you. I didn't know what you had seen. I didn't know if you would tell her . . .'

Marian said, 'I didn't know who he was.'

'I never saw him again, I need hardly say. The moment he got back on dry land they drove him off to Falmouth, and he was gone. Stella didn't say a word to him. Only looked at him, and touched his hand. And she couldn't forgive me. She hated the sight of me after that. I had to move out.'

'But can you wonder? You had done such a terrible thing . . .'

'You did see, then?'

'Oh yes, I saw.'

'Did you tell your mother?'

'No.'

'Thank God for that. I could never tell if Stella knew. She seemed not to – she never reproached me with *that*. Only with neglecting you. But I've always been troubled about it.'

'You deserve to have been,' said Marian.

'Ah – you are more like your mother than at first appears. Of course, she was right in a way. She kept saying I should have watched what you were doing. She couldn't forgive me.'

'All this time, I've thought it was Stella I was with. And I thought it was a stranger who rescued me.'

'I'm sorry. I really am. But don't waste any grief on your father; he was trash, really. Pathetic. Just your mother's bit of rough.'

'What do you mean?' cried Marian, standing up, crying out. 'How can you say that? He was trash, although if Stella had him, you wanted him? You mean he would fuck any slut who made passes at him?'

'Sit down,' said Violet with sudden force. 'Keep your voice down. You should forgive us for *that*. I did make passes at him. But it was the war. I had just lost my lover. He was famished. We were young. And we were afraid of dying.'

Into a long silence Marian said, 'Yes, I forgive you. But I can't eat another mouthful. I will pay the bill, and get them to call a taxi to take you home. But you must tell me what you meant when you said my father was trash.'

'His own people despised him. He had let another man go out in his place and be drowned.'

Later, Marian sat in the window, looking at the lights of the town jewelling the darkness, and musing. It was an immense relief to her that it had not been Stella's fault. However unkind Stella had been to Violet, by Violet's account of things, it had not been Stella who had exposed Marian to the naked sight of copulation, or to the rising tide. Marian wondered with anguish whether the suppressed, the obliterated, belief that it had been Stella at the mouth of the cave had coloured her feelings for Stella subliminally all her life – is this why she had been so quickly resentful, so demanding? If so it was now too late to confess, to explain, to make amends.

But Marian also felt joy. For Violet's photograph had shown her what she had not managed otherwise to know – shown her an expression on her young mother's face that she never remembered, later, having seen. Somehow she had managed not to know how greatly Stella had loved her.

And with all this it was only much later, when she was on her way to bed, that it came to her that she knew now exactly why Thomas Tremorvah might have lied to her, might say he had never been to Kynance.

The house stood open to the soft air of a late autumn day. For the time of year it was astonishingly warm; the front door stood wide, admitting a sloping parallelogram of light and heat, bisecting the hall, and dividing the shabby carpet into plots of light and dark. From the sitting room window a few people could be seen swimming from the beach; a few children running in the waves' edge, one or two bright encampments of grown-ups. The sea wore azure, edged with turquoise, and fringed with pearly white. The escallonia hedge that screened the house front from the road seeped its hot spicy odour into the garden. A faint haze stood on the view, making it seem to have been drawn in chalk, rather than in oils.

Leo came in without knocking. He had a video tape in his hand. 'I've borrowed this for you,' he said to Marian. 'Can I stay and watch it too? – I've never seen it.'

'What is it, Leo?'

'Barry Cockcroft's film – or a tape of it, rather. He lent it to me.'

'Film of what? And who is Barry Cockcroft?'

'He's a writer and film director. Lives in St Ives, now. He made a film way back, somewhere in the seventies, I think, about the lifeboats in St Ives. The thing is, when he made the film William Freeman was still alive, and so was the man you were asking about – the one who wouldn't go. The problem is, I've only got this for twenty-four hours. It's his only copy, and he has to show it to someone tomorrow night.'

'Well, what's wrong with now, Leo? Put it on now.'

A few seconds of black and white flicker – 'random noise' Donald had called it, the background rustle of the molecular dance of the universe – then a title *Take a Lifejacket* – the room was too bright, the picture dimmed by contrast, so Marian got up and drew the curtains across the shimmering day. As she went back to her chair Alice slipped into the room, and sat on the floor.

'What are we watching?' she asked.

'Shut up and see,' said Leo cheerfully. 'You too, Toby?' For Toby was leaning against the door to the hall.

'I'm going out,' said Toby. 'I'm waiting for Matthew,' but for the moment he stood where he was.

The film began telling the now familiar terrible story of the 1939 calamity. But it ranged about. It told a hair-raising story of a rescue from Hell's Mouth. Some potholers had got into trouble in the shaft, and had to be rescued from the sea-cave below. A lifeboat man had paddled into the cave in his lifejacket – he said cheerfully he couldn't swim – and tied the stranded climbers one by one, in lifejackets, to a line. '*They came out like tin cans, floating . . .*'

'That's Dan Paynter!' said Matthew. He had appeared beside Toby in the door. He sat down beside Alice, all intention of going out suspended.

The same thing had threatened to happen again, the video told them. *What did you think when you seemed to be going out for a repeat?* asked Barry Cockcroft's voice.

'Shook. Fright. Everybody gets frighted when them rockets go – well I do, I'm only speaking for myself. I uster shake.'

And now the camera shows William Freeman, telling his story of the 1939 disaster. *Just as I got there a man gave his jacket up, and the coxswain said, "I want somebody to go."*

'I said, "Well all right. I'll go. I'll do." "All right," he said. "You'll do." So I went right then and accepted the jacket on.'

'Did you know that man?' the voice asked.

'Ess, I knew him, but he was an older man than me. I suppose he thought it might have been too much for him, you know. I knew him well, ess, he was a fisherman.'

'In this community,' said Barry Cockcroft's quiet voice, *'that must have been a hard decision to take. Who was that man?'*

'I don't think you ought to say the man's name, do you?' said William Freeman.

'I shouldn't,' said Margaret Freeman, a much younger Margaret Freeman, sitting on the arm of her husband's chair. *'He's a cousin of mine too, and he might not like it.'*

Toby said to Matthew, 'Do you know about this, Mathy?'

'Not all. Not like this,' said Mathy. 'The old people talk about it, but they don't say it all.'

Now the film was showing them an old man, mending nets. Sitting at a window, high up, with a bobbin in his hands, knotting and mending nets. John Stevens. He is telling his story. He went down to help with the launch.

'It was blowing a ninety mile an hour gale. Well, I said, this is going to be a job. She's only going to be half manned today. Second cox, he never heard the rockets at all. Anyway, I dressed to go in her. I wasn't one of the regular crew — she had a regular crew at that time. Anyway, I went down, and when I found out where she was going I thought t'myself she'll never get there, fourteen mile to west of the Head. The sand from Porthmeor was blowing over all the houses onto the lifeboat slip. So I thought, I'll give them a hand to launch.

'But when I passed the light, and my brother-in-law seen me, he said, "John," he said, "go with us, will you?" I could see there was only four men there. So then the coxswain came around the bow of her, he said, "Govn'er go with us, will ee?" I said, "All right, I'll go." I was thinking that he wouldn't put her outside of the bay. And I went aboard to take this jacket, the life-jacket was on the deck, so I took it, and it was like a lump of lead in my hands, when they're only featherweight. I was going to start to put it on, or go over the side to put it on, but as I neared the side of the boat there was voices in my two ears, "drop that jacket, drop that jacket," incessant, incessant, which stopped me. Yes, I've heard them before, my angels. But they were distinct voices, because I wanted to put that jacket on. So then I had the courage to say to the coxswain, I said, "Bar, you give this jacket to somebody else."'

And now some reconstruction. Teams of men by torch-light, towing the boat across the harbour beach in two long lines, going up to their necks in the water . . . and Margaret Freeman saying, 'Couldn't see the sea — it was all white like soapsuds as far as the eye could see . . .'

'So I give them a hand to launch the boat,' John Stevens was saying, 'and she turned around and went over all that broken water like a flying bird, and that was the end of her.'

There was a sort of stillness in Marian. The room was quiet, the children, Leo, Matthew, all held to attention.

A light breeze fluttered the edge of the curtain at the open window. William Freeman's voice was telling them what happened in the boat, how it had gone over and over, how he had heard one man shouting to them in the dark, how he had fetched up alone in the empty boat on the far side of the bay, and blundered around for help . . .

But Marian was not thinking about the ordeal of those who went with the boat, but about this other man, who did not. As though you had been looking for something for a long time, for years, and when you found it, when it was apparent you were about to find it, you were afraid. You were circling round and round, and the nearer you came to the heart of it, the less you could bear the thought of the stillness within it, what you would know when you stood still.

The film was telling her that William Freeman had never set foot in a boat again. He had been brought home in a terrible state. *'Fact, I don't go near the water any more, now,'* he was saying. *'Not further than the top of the pier. Strange thing – there was a boat going out one day there, and I was looking out, and she was rolling a bit as she was going out. And you know I had to turn away, I felt sick!'* He was laughing, bewildered at himself, *'And I was only on the pier! Ess . . .'*

'Oh, I didn't ask the right questions!' Marian thought. For what can it have been like with a family to look after, and a child sick, and the breadwinner unable to work? How had they managed? What was the price paid for that one night?

Barry Cockcroft was asking if William Freeman ever talked to the other man about it.

'No. Never. I don't talk about it to anyone.'

'What do you say when you meet him?'

'*Meet him? Oh, nothing. Just pass on. Never say anything to him, just pass on.*'

Marian got up. You long for something, and then you turn away from it. She had seen how nearly this touched her; she had begun to guess her own story. And at the last minute you flinch away . . . She left the room.

Leo found her a little later, in the garden. She was finding the curious double-edged quality of the beauty of the place. The haze had lifted, and you could see distance and distance beyond Godrevy all the way to Trevose. The horizon was drawn in a clear dark line, floating on a paler stripe of shining water, as though it belonged to the sky as much as to the water. If you had the least joy to bring to it, this spectacle lifted your heart; if you were in any darkness it sharpened the mental pain.

'Leo,' she said, 'that London dealer told me about a lot of backbiting and quarrelling among the artists here. He made it sound terrible. I wondered how true it was . . .'

'Well, yes and no. I mean they did quarrel. In-fighting was meat and drink to some of them, who shall be nameless, although they are famous. But there's another side to it.'

'Like what?'

'Kindness. Fellow feeling. I'm not the only nipper who got a helping hand, a box of crayons, free lessons. They shared with each other what they had; a hot meal, a warm fireside for someone half dead of hunger and cold. Given a little money, they bought each other's pictures out of friendship, and gave them back without a murmur if a richer buyer appeared. They worked and talked all day and all night. And if they quarrelled it was because they cared about it all so much.'

'I see,' she said.

'Do you? People said we quarrelled about nothing, because they don't think art matters. It wasn't nothing to us, it was everything. Different things matter to different people, don't you think? Or why would you walk out in the middle of watching that video? Look, we're all going down for a drink. I've left the tape in the machine. I'll come back for it later.'

You had to concede to Leo, she realized, an instinct for what to do.

Going down the hill together, Alice put her arm through Leo's. Toby and Mathy were walking together, deep in talk. As they went down Lifeboat Hill they picked up Bish and Bar, who were chatting by the propped boards offering fishing trips round the bay. At the foot of Custom House Passage Mathy split off, and rejoined them at the door of the Sloop with Ann. They piled into the pub, and settled round a table in the furthest room, where the sketches of local characters petered out, and were adulterated with one or two consciously arty nudes.

Toby noticed, with mild incredulity, that Leo and Alice were holding hands under the table, and illogically emboldened, reached likewise under the table for Ann's.

'Town has gone down dreadful, if you ask me,' said an elderly man perched on a bar stool within earshot.

'What d'ye mean, gone down, Uncle?' said Ann.

'Last fifteen year, St Ives has gone down to nothing. Uster be a queue to get into chapel at half-past five on Sundays,' he answered her. 'Now you can go down at ten to six and get a seat.'

'Well, it used to be you wouldn't find a Methodist in the Sloop, come to that,' said Mathy cheerfully. 'Can I buy you a drink?'

'Thank'ee no,' said Uncle. 'I got this one, and I know my limitations.'

'That film we were watching . . .' said Toby.

'If you want to know more about it,' Mathy said, 'those old boys in the public bar remember about it, I expect.'

'I wouldn't know what to ask,' said Toby. 'But that man who thought they shouldn't have gone – he was right in a way, wasn't he?'

'No, he wadn't!' said Mathy, with sudden passion. 'You couldn't have that, boy. You couldn't have people getting in and out of a boat, and arguing with the coxswain. If you're down to go, you go. Couldn't ever get her launched else.'

'They had to be very brave.'

'No,' said Mathy again. 'It idn't brave. It got to be considered a normal thing to do. Can't have people thinking, well I don't be no hero . . . 'As to be, well, automatic.'

Uncle at the bar chipped in. 'I've heard Dan Paynter tell how he come home on leave in the war – just a three-day leave, mind, and as he come down Skidden Hill, right off the train, the rockets went up, and so he goes straight out in the boat, leaving his kit bag in the shed without his family so much as knowing he was back.'

It came suddenly to Toby that if every life involved moral dice-playing, then he knew which risks he himself wanted to take.

'Mathy,' he said, 'if I lived here, could I be in the lifeboat?'

Up the hill, back at the house, Marian picked up one of the photographs on her bedside table, frame and all, and got into the car to drive herself to Gwithian. It seemed a long way. The road was up in Carbis Bay, and two buses coming opposite ways were in difficulty getting past each other. It had become a crisp and very clear day, the kind of day that transforms suburbs into bright utopias, their gardens into toy parks. As the road turned and descended through Lelant, the sweeping and curving profile of the hill with its stand of dark Scotch pines seen over the old houses by the road, offered her sea-struck eyes a reminder of inland beauty. And then – it seemed characteristic of the place – she drove past the junk hoardings of the pleasure park, and the dressed up person, presumably a desperate person, disguised as a wizard, and waving a wand of welcome. So into Hayle and Copperhouses, and out to Gwithian, and onto the Towans.

Marian rang the door bell of Captain Tremorvah's cabin, and waited. The tide was out, and the beach wide. A bitterly cold wind swept the shore. She looked at the girdle of wall round the abandoned garden on Godrevy, and picked out the outhouses, the flights of steps, the ruined post of the breeches buoy. It brought over her that curious ache that abandoned habitations of all kinds arouse – that foolish desire to repossess, to re-roof, to weed and restore, and resume the once viable pattern of days. You would need a boat, you would need a telephone . . . The glazed door behind her opened, and Captain Tremorvah was standing there.

'Can I come in?' said Marian.

He stepped back. She entered the porch, and this time he retreated into the room behind, and she followed. His living room surprised her, though she saw at once that it should not have done. It was very tidy and clean. A bright little enamel stove fed from a polished copper coal-scuttle kept it warm. The windows were double-glazed. There were two dark red leather wing armchairs, and a settee with an oriental rug cast over it. The walls were covered with admiralty charts, and photographs of ships in bird's-eye maple frames. A barometer and a ship's clock shared a corner of wall beside a door to the kitchen. Marian's eye was caught at once by a row of medals with their ribbons, pinned to a velvet pad, framed and hung up above the elaborately decorated harmonium, complete with music stool and built in candelabra, which dominated the far wall. A plate-rack ran round the room at picture-rail level, carrying a procession of rather good Chinese porcelain blue and white plates.

Marian was making a rapid reassessment. She had associated living in a wooden cabin on the Towans, if it was not as a holiday home, with poverty. The evident prosperity of the room turned the choice of house – well you could hardly call such a hut a house – into an eccentricity. He was silent, just looking at her.

'I brought this to show you,' she said, pulling the photograph out of her bag, and handing it to him. 'Look, these are my children, Alice and Toby. Toby is the spitting image of your grand-nephew Matthew Vanson. They might almost be twins, don't you think?'

He looked at the photograph. 'I couldn't tell you,' he said, handing it back. 'I've never seen my grand-nephew. Never clapped eyes on him.'

She was baffled. 'He lives in Downalong,' she said. 'I don't know which street.'

'I haven't set foot in St Ives since the day I left,' he said.

'When was that?' she asked. 'When did you leave?'

'Nineteen forty-one. Joined the navy.'

'I was two, then. You must remember me. Don't you want to see your grandchildren?'

He did not answer, but she saw his eyes go to the photograph she was still holding. She didn't know what to say to him, standing there old and frail, and denying it, denying her. She was ashamed of herself for insisting, for bullying a frail old man, with his watery dark eyes, the irises clouded with encroaching white. She thought she ought to leave it, she had come too late, he was too old for such upheavals now.

But, 'Captain Tremorvah,' she heard herself saying, 'that night in 1939, where were you when they launched the boat?'

'Can you walk?' he said. 'Come out and I'll show you something.'

He put on a navy greatcoat, taking it from a hook behind the door. It seemed somewhat too big for him, and he hunched himself into it, as though expecting, when he opened the back door, a mighty wind. And there was indeed a smart breeze blowing off the bay. He crossed the road at once, and led her on a track towards the beach. And facing this way the opposite side of the bay was spread out in view, all the way to Clodgy Point, and you could see the whole town of St Ives, clinging to its sloping hills. You could see the harbour, and the golden crescent moons of the beaches – where was the Island? Marian wondered, and then a patch of cloud-shadow moved a little and the emerald green cushion of the Island slopes came clear to her. But Captain Tremorvah plunged on, and she had to follow.

The path led to the brink of quite a high sandy cliff, instead of a slope to the sands. Half broken concrete steps had been laid in it, and then subverted by the undercut of wind and tide, but they scrambled down. Then they were walking briskly on the enormous shore. The tide had drawn far back, and was piling what seemed like a tumbling vertical wall of wave on breaking wave onto the sand without advancing. So flat was the great beach that it had not drained dry with the ebb, but was glossed with a huge expanse of standing water, reflecting the sky. It had a lilac-grey silken light on it, in which the white tower of the lighthouse was reflected like a dangling satin ribbon, shimmering gently in the wind. Mirrored opalescent clouds paddled in the inch-deep lake, and the two of them strode through it, walking on water like latter-day miracle workers.

He led her straight towards the lighthouse. On their right the little plain behind a sand bar where the Red River spilled out to the sea gave way to the whale-backed height of the headland, bright green grass-cover mantling black cliffs of rock, spines and plateaux of rock jutting across the sands to the water's edge. Above them some people walked, some cars were parked, and as they came to the foot of the cliffs the river was running across their way. It spread out, and divided and converged, playing a game of delta from a geography book, all in miniature across the sands, but it was fast running and quite deep.

Captain Tremorvah simply chose a fairly shallow point and strode across – he was wearing boots – but Marian had to take off her shoes, pull off her tights, hitch her skirt, and wade across, near to knee deep in freezing water. And then the sand gave way to the rocks, and she had to stop and put her shoes back on her wet and sandy feet. She sat down to the job, and when she had laced her shoes again, her companion had disappeared. She clambered after him, and saw him still steadily advancing, clambering over the rough, seaweedy, rock-pool-cradling uncovered bedrock of the land.

He stopped quite suddenly, and she came up to him. They were very near the lighthouse, almost at the edge of the wide bay, where the strait between shore and light-house was at its narrowest, looking due westwards to the piles of rock on Clodgy Point, standing in outline against the afternoon light. They were on a platform of rock, deeply creviced and cracked, but fairly level. Below them another such crazed level extended a little way.

'D'you see that?' he said.

She looked down at the rocks, following where he pointed. 'What?' she said.

'That iron there. D'you see?'

Wedged hard in the rocks was a rusty iron spar, worn and eroded, and pitted, as bright orange as the patches of lichen that clung to the rock higher up.

'What is it?' she asked. She wouldn't have given it a second glance, had she walked there alone.

'That's her keel,' he said. 'That's where I should have fetched up. With the rest. I should have fetched up there.'

'If you had been in the boat, you mean?'

'Had I done what I should have done, had my wicked-ness not prevented me. See, the sea took that boat clean across the bay, turning her over and over, and it cast her down so hard just here that her keel is fixed in those rocks as long as that iron lasts. I'm fetched up here too, now, as long as I shall last. And no argument.'

'Have you never wished to go home?' she asked him.

'It's an unforgiving place,' he said. 'Or, it was to me. I

speak only as I find. And I've got as close as I can come. We must walk back now, before the sea takes back the sand, and makes us go the long way round.'

'But you can see it all, from here!' she exclaimed, watching the sunlight sweep across the distance, brightening everything below the softly outlined hills, and racing across the bay towards them, chasing the inky blue of the sea in cloud-shadow, and making it lucent azure.

'Yes,' he said. 'Trencrom Hill, Trink Hill, Knill's Steeple, Rosewall Hill, Clodgy Point, Man's Head, the Island, Porthminster Point, Carrack Gladden, Lelant Church . . . I can see them. And all the town. I can see the roof of my mother's house from here, and the roof of the house where I was when I should have been down to the boat.'

'You were with my mother.'

'I must go in,' he said. 'There's a chill on the wind.'

They walked back in silence, along the roaring waves, in silence forded the icy stream, Marian once again needing to wade barefoot, recovered the distance, clambered the sandy cleft in the cliffs, and stood once more at his door. He held it open for her, and she stepped into the porch.

'I mustn't tread sand in,' she said. She had become very cold, to the point of trembling, and her toes were numb in her sand-laden shoes.

'Sit in that chair,' he said. He hung up his coat, and went indoors. And in a short while came out to her with a basin of water. He put the bowl at her feet, and said, 'Take off your shoes.'

It was barely warm water, but it stung her. The sand drifted off her feet to the bottom of the bowl. He brought an enamel jug to her, and added hotter water. And then more. Her feet stopped tingling, and felt part of her again.

She moved her toes. The comfortable warmth spread through her. He stooped in front of her, holding a towel in his hands, steadying himself on the arm of her chair, and began to dry her feet. She was embarrassed, she nearly stopped him doing it, but some instinct stilled her.

'You can come in now,' he said.

He had put her shoes in front of the stove, with news-paper thrust in them. She sat in one of the red chairs, and he brought hot black tea, and sat in the other. As once, long ago, he had put her down freezing beside the fire . . . There was a long silence in the room. She would not ask him anything more. She was bringing herself round to not needing to.

'Round two in the morning,' he said. 'The rocket went up round two in the morning. And I wasn't where I ought to have been. We was like two birds in a nest that nobody knew about, and I was naked as the day I was born. Well, I heard the rocket, and I jumped out of bed at once, and began to put my clothes on, quick as I could. And there was all this uproar in the street. People running on the cobbles. You could hear them above the wind and the storm and everything. I was stood inside the front door, aheaving my jacket on, and there was a fixed bit of window above the door, and I saw the light from the street-lamp just outside cast against the wall, and the foot-falls clattering on the cobbles outside, and I realized I couldn't go out. Not without being seen. I was trapped in there, behind that door. So I waited for things to quiet down, and the coming and going to be over, and I waited till nearly morning. It was morning till men stopped going up and down to the Island to look out and see if they could see any sign of the boat. She was launched and she was lost before I could go out in the air.'

'But there aren't any cobbles by Stella's house, and it

isn't on the way to the Island,' said Marian, 'I don't understand you.'

'Her first house in St Ives. She had a cottage and a loft in Bethesda Hill. She moved higher up the town a bit later, to keep out of sight a bit. But she was in Downalong, then. I only had to slip round the corner from my mother's house, and go through the cellar door, and I was there.'

'And you had been lovers for a while, by then?'

'Fornicators, yes.'

'Why didn't you marry?'

'Couldn't. I had a wife at that time. She was in the sanatorium, very poorly, yes. And times were hard. Your mother put an advert in the *St Ives Times* for a model, for a man to be a drawing model, for half a crown. And I needed the money. I hurt my hand on a fish-hook, and I was off the boats till it mended, so I needed the money. She had me take my clothes off to draw me, and I thought, well, I would. I had a devil in me, a bit of a swagger, you know, and I thought it wouldn't do no harm. She was a handsome woman, your mother. And I was stood there, cock-naked. So then I was a deep dyed sinner all in a minute and I hardly knew how it happened.'

'But – it can't have been just once, surely?'

'Once we started we couldn't leave off. She got in my blood and bones so I couldn't think of anything else. But we kept it dark. We kept it secret. I don't know what my brothers would have done to me, what my mother would have said if they'd known, but there it was. They didn't. And I thought I was getting away with it, I thought even God didn't see, till that night. Even then I didn't appreciate what had happened, at first. Because it does occur sometimes, missing the boat. Not everybody gets down there every time the rocket goes up. You'd have a bit of explaining to do, and then they'd rib you a bit, and forget it. So when I got out that morning I thought I'd think of something to say, some sort of a reason where I was, and it would be soon forgotten. The hand of God had struck me in my wickedness, and I didn't even feel the force of it at first.'

He got up, and felt how her shoes were doing, drying out beside the stove. He replaced them in the warmth, and went on speaking, though perhaps not really to her. 'Well, it didn't die down. It went on and on, recriminations. And everyone counting the regular crew on their fingers and saying where were you? And how come you wasn't there? The second cox, he didn't hear the rockets, but there were some that didn't believe him. I could walk round the town and feel like a stinking fish, the way people looked at me. All those widows and orphans. There were those two men walking round the town, one of them broken in health, and the other cold-shouldered, and both on my conscience.'

'But why—'

'They were neither of them regular jacket-holders. They were both volunteers. If there hadn't been places in the boat that wouldn't have happened not to one or the other of them.'

'But my mother didn't give you the cold-shoulder – not for that?'

'I couldn't hardly stand the sight of her after that night, I was so ashamed. She moved up the hill a bit, so I could go to her along the back of the beach, and up the path out of sight, but I only went once or twice. I couldn't stand the thought that people might guess what had kept me from my duty. So anyway, September nineteen forty-one my poor wife died, and I got out of it into the navy.'

'Did you keep in touch with my mother? Did you write?'

'She wrote. I kept the letter.'

'But she thought you were dead.'

'She was better off without me. I was no good to a decent woman.'

'You had a child, too. There's no such thing as a decent child. What about me?'

'I couldn't be trusted with you,' he said. 'There at Kynance . . .'

'You reached me in time,' she said.

'Only just. Another split second or two . . . I used to dream about that. In a ship under fire at sea, I would dream about that. I was on a destroyer that got torpedoed in the North Atlantic. An Icelander pulled me out of the drink – a trawler. There was only a few of us rescued. So I thought Stella would read in the papers the loss of the ship. And if I didn't write again she would be free of me. I wasn't any good to her.'

'That letter—'

He got up, and went to the roll-top desk in the corner, and raised the lid. He opened one of the multiple little drawers, and brought her a small, stained, folded paper. Something fell out of it as she opened it. A photograph. It fell face down, and she saw the censor's stamp on the back. It was of herself, standing holding a wooden spoon beside a sandcastle. And the letter was in Stella's writing.

Dearest Tommy Mackerel,
This is a quick note to tell you that I am leaving St Ives. Our girl is very pretty and happy, and has made friends of some of the Vanson children. She looks very like one of them – Becky, I think, roughly her age. The thing is people have noticed, people are beginning to talk. With you away I can't talk it over with anyone, but I know you would hate it all to come out in your absence, so I shall have to find some-

*where else to live. I'll send you the new address as soon as
we are settled. Don't be brave – take care of yourself – love
always – Stella*

'And afterwards? After you were rescued? You were
brave though she asked you not to be, I see.' Marian
pointed at the row of medals.

'I wasn't much worth preserving,' he said. 'But the Lord
didn't see fit to take me to him. I served in the navy and
the merchant navy, and got to be a captain.'

'And then you came home here?'

'Within sight of home, yes. Fetched up where I should
have fetched up in the first place. But it pleases the Lord
to keep me waiting.'

The pattern in Marian's mind was moving like cloud-
shadow – as the past came clear the present was cast into
gloom. She folded the letter carefully, and put it back on
the desk. She took her shoes from the grate, pulled the
paper out of them, and put them on.

'Father,' she said, almost stumbling on the unfamiliar
word, 'would you like me to come again?'

'You remind me of your mother,' he said. 'I don't need
that.'

White with sudden anger she said, 'In all those years did
it never occur to you that *I* might need *you*?'

But the moment these words were spoken, they were
empty. Poor man, she thought, I come as a shock to him.
Give him time, he hasn't much left. Even the longest tide
turns eventually; her need for him which had been
ebbing all her life had reached its turn while she was
standing there, and the coming flood would be his need
of her.

'Would you like to keep the photograph?' she asked,
holding it out to him.

'What are their names?' he asked her, taking it.

'Alice, and Toby,' she told him. 'And they loved Stella dearly.'

The house seemed yawningly empty when she returned. She would have started to tell them at once, pouring out the news of their grandfather, had they been there. But she had learned to be alone. She made herself a cup of tea, surveyed the supper supplies and decided to go out, watched the rapid sunset extinguish itself over the bay. Then she rewound the tape in the video recorder, and sat down to watch the last few minutes, the bit she had fled from before.

And now the quiet voice was asking John Stevens, *'Did anyone ever say anything to you about it?'*

'Never.'

'So the fact that you took your jacket off has never been mentioned to you by any of the other fishermen in St Ives?'

'No. Nobody's never said a word or raised it to me. And do you know, me and Freeman, we won't even look at – speak to each other. We haven't spoken to each other since. Because of memories.'

And yet somehow, with some triumph of tact and skill, the producer had contrived it. For now the screen shows her Doble's Wall, along the Harbour Wharf, and Mount Zion behind it. And the two old men were meeting – John Stevens going up the steeply sloping street, William Freeman coming down it.

'How are you?' John Stevens asks.

'All right.'

'You aren't too good . . .'

'No. No breath . . .'

'This is nearly thirty-seven or eight years since we've spoken to each other. Not for any reason . . .'

'No, no.'

'Whenever I see you I get full of emotion.'

And William Freeman asks, 'Why, John? Why should it be? We aren't here long enough for that.'

'I get emotional . . .'

'Ess . . .'

'The thoughts do travel back, understand? See?'

And as the film ended the two of them were leaning on Doble's Wall, looking at the harbour, and talking about the price of fish. It had been staged; of course it was staged, and yet . . .

The children had returned, were standing in the room with her, and Marian found herself crying, the long dammed-up tears flowing freely down her cheeks.

Toby said, 'You know, Mum, what people cannot bear to remember, surely they should just forget.'

She thought about that the next day, walking out along the cliff path. A young man's perception; with a gust of affection for him, she saw that it sprang from an un-damaged mind, from an assumption that forgetfulness was possible, could even be a deliberate act. Perhaps he needed to think that now. Later he would know, like anyone else, that as life lengthens you cannot forget without un-ravelling yourself. The details flow away, and rearrange themselves like sands on the wind, and leave the bones of recollection like black rocks standing naked on a beach. She needed to think something through, to catch the train of thought that connected forgetting with forgiving, but first she had to think about Toby.

'I could stay here for ever,' she had said to him, standing in the bay window, and looking at the sweep of the sea below them.

'What's stopping you?' he had asked.

'Well, for one thing, being too far from my children,' she had said, meaning to stop the idea short.

'You wouldn't be too far from me, Ma,' he said. 'I've packed it in, in London.'

'Was that wise? Explain to me.'

'Well, it would have been hard to go on as a trader once there was a shadow on one's name. And they cast a shadow on everyone they suspended. They haven't any evidence against me. They know perfectly well if they threw the book at me I could name others – some of them rather high in the firm. So I've been negotiating with them on the phone. I exploited the situation, and collected a nice little kitty. Redundancy money, if you like. I'll be quite comfortable for a while.'

She thought about it. 'I think you must be telling me that you did it, really.'

'I'm afraid so, Ma. And it leaves a nasty taste. That's why I'm throwing it in.'

'But what will you do?'

'Sell the London flat, buy a cottage in Downalong, and help Mathy finance a boat,' he said briskly. 'Keep out of harm's way. I can't get into trouble doing that. I'm going up to London on the sleeper tonight to fix things.'

She had thought about it. 'But in the long run?' she had asked him. 'You always planned to be rich. You were so fond of the good things in life—'

'I've rather changed my mind', he said, 'about what those good things are.'

'I'd be a long way from Alice, though,' she had said, jumping back several moves in the conversation.

'Ma, I wouldn't rely on Alice,' he had said. 'She might be anywhere.'

Alone in the house that night, Marian set herself to the task of thinking. She could tell herself her story now. 'My father was a fisherman, my mother was an artist,' seemed a St Ives sort of thing to have happened. And in that place and time it needed to be kept secret. Perhaps Stella's friends would have been tolerant, perhaps they wouldn't. Perhaps it would have seemed shocking to get into a liaison with one's model – well, no, hardly that – but then perhaps if the model was the man – would it perhaps have been shocking to cross the gulf of class, and risk ill feeling with the deeply religious local people? Anyway, for what-ever reason, Stella had kept it secret. Even her friends of that time, even Violet who had lived with her, had not known until much later who Marian's father was.

And father had been deeply shamed by it. He had been kept from doing his duty by it. Perhaps he had got religion only much later in life, but even at the time he had suffered sharp remorse. And it was to protect him that Stella had left the town, taken her daughter away, escaped from rumour and guesswork. And Marian saw, suddenly clair-voyant, that it had not been the fear that her father would be unmasked as an adulterer that had displaced them, but the far worse fear that it might be guessed where he had been that night. That others would accuse him of what now he accused himself of – being to blame for what happened when the boat was being launched short-handed.

It had been a very damaging thing for Stella to do, going elsewhere. She had lost touch with the golden vein of inspiration that had given her her best work. She had not been able to paint like that anywhere else. All the best things she had done depended on the light here, on the land here, on the moving water, on the circle of other artists, on the ramshackle warren of studios, on love and anger and rivalry and the bright tide of ideas. Stella had needed the talk, the work to look at, the winds of influence that outsiders brought with them to blow around the town. Exile had hurt her badly. So why, when she thought that Thomas Tremorvah was dead, had Stella not come back again here?

But by then, of course, the people were dispersed, the scene was different. The Society of Artists was split from top to bottom, the modernists had resigned and made their own society, and that too was rent by dissension. You make choices and live with them. Your chances don't come twice. And Marian's chance to talk to Stella, to understand her, had gone for good.

She heard the front door softly opened, and softly closed and bolted. Alice, coming in very late. Perhaps it was unconsciously waiting for Alice that kept Marian awake, thinking. You never get over being parent-figure when they are under the same roof. Ridiculous, Marian told herself, I wouldn't worry if she were anywhere else. The bedroom door opened, and Alice looked round it. Alice flushed, and dishevelled, and glowing.

'I saw your light still on,' she said, coming to sit on the end of the bed.

'Hullo, darling,' said Marian. 'Do you want to come and meet your grandfather tomorrow?'

'Whenever,' said Alice, 'but not tomorrow. Mum, I'm going to the Scillies for a few days. Leo's taking me; he's going to show me a few things.'

Marian said, 'Alice, what can you be playing at? Shouldn't you keep company with someone nearer your own age?'

'Keep company? Mother, this isn't about sex.'

'But I thought . . .' Marian foundered, visibly astonished.

'Well, it *is*,' said Alice, 'but only for comfort. Only out of kindness. It doesn't matter. It's your generation that is so hung up about sex . . .'

'But, my God, child, Leo *is* my generation; even older!'

'Oh, I see,' said Alice. 'I assumed it was me you were worrying about.'

'Make no mistake, I do worry about you. Deeply. I hate to see you so unhappy.'

'You would rather see me happily married with two point eight children and a nice little job as a music teacher? You would, wouldn't you?'

'Would that be so bad a thing?'

'It seems impossible, that's all,' said Alice, suddenly quiet. 'I have plenty of offers, Mum. But I can't love anyone who puts love first.'

'But Alice that's what love is like. Any kind of love. I have put you and Toby first from the moment you were born.'

'And didn't you ever think it might be the wrong place to put children? That it might ask too much of us? That it was hard enough finding our own reason for living, without being yours as well? Look, I'll be off very early; we have to catch the boat. So here's the key to Leo's. He says go and look at the work. OK?'

Alice leaned over Marian and kissed her. 'There, Mum, don't look sad. I hate you to look sad.'

And yet sadness possessed her. She woke the next morning to an empty house, almost audibly empty, and out of a clear dream. Marian did not usually remember dreams, and hated to be told other people's, but this one lingered in hallucinatory clarity. She had been going to see Stella in the Barrington house. She had let herself in, and marched straight to the barn at the back. 'Mother,' she had said, 'you never told me that you loved my father. You never said there was anything for which you risked your art.'

Stella made no reply to this, but began to fade away among the stacked canvases, the shadows in the dark barn.

And dream, Marian began wailing, 'Why didn't you tell me? I got you wrong! Why didn't you tell me?'

And as she woke an unspoken voice said to her clearly in the silence, 'Why didn't you ask?'

Slowly, like a person maimed, she got herself dressed, and went into the breakfast room.

The table was laid, and there were two notes leaning against the milk jug. One from Toby saying, 'Back tomorrow. Love, T.' One from Alice saying, 'Sorry about last night. I take it all back. Love, Alice.'

But also, bursting suddenly into the kitchen through the back door, came Alice – a radiant Alice with her duffel bag in one hand and a ripped-open envelope in the other.

'I thought you'd gone,' said Marian.

'Oh, God, Mum, I nearly missed it!' said Alice. 'I just passed the postman on my way down the hill, and I just happened to ask him if he had a letter for me—'

'But what is it?' asked Marian.

'From Max. A rehearsal tonight. I've come back for my viola, and I can just about get the morning train. Max wants me back! Make me a quick coffee, Mum, will you?'

'Alice, what about Leo?'

'I'll phone him. Don't worry, Mum, he's going to the Scillies anyway. He'll get over it.'

Marian made the coffee. She heard Alice on the phone in the hall – a brutally quick and unemotional conversation – and then she reappeared, holding her instrument case.

'Alice, wait,' cried Marian, as Alice opened the door to go. 'Are you sure you ought to go running back to Max at the crook of his little finger?'

'It isn't *Max*, Mum, it's music,' she said. 'And don't forget to look at Leo's work,' she called, slamming the door behind her.

So later, when she had made her bed, and cleared her breakfast dishes, Marian went out. She took the route down Tregenna Hill, with unfolding prospects of the bay and harbour. The town was basking in unseasonable light, tricking itself out in gold and azure. It did not cheer her. She looked at it with bitter regret, engulfed as it was by vulgarity, by the blaring music from the amusement arcade, and the stupid posters, by the junk art and junk food on offer everywhere. The peeling paint, the stonecrop-blocked gutters with the green slick on the walls below them, the signs all there if you were in the mood for them, of decay, of enterprises fallen on hard times, appeared in uncanny clarity to her as she passed. The fishermen's lodges on the wharf were all locked up and empty, and nobody leaned on the railings beside them to exchange the time of day.

Marian walked with leaden feet into Downalong. Here more than anywhere you could feel the force of a way of life that had ebbed away like a neap tide. This place was shaped for people who all knew each other, whose doors stood open to their neighbours, who for good or ill lived full in each other's view. The generations of their families had piled up here like the sands on the shore. They had worked together, and shared the sea's bounty and the sea's dangers. The lifeboat had been their form of manliness, their form of solidarity, their fashion of loving their fellow men. And the lovely old times were gone like the masted ships in the harbour, and the shoals in the sea. *There is nothing whatever do not look like what it was* . . . Look at it now, she thought, the people dispersed, their livelihood withered away, the survivors prised out of their houses to make way for the mobs of visitors—

The nearer she got to Leo's door the more slowly she walked. She was afraid; she dreaded it, she was half drowned already. She realized, standing there with the key in her hand, that Leo must be the real thing, or she would not be afraid of his work. But having come so far, with such inner difficulty, she opened the door, and went in.

There was a bronze wave on a stone plinth. It was polished, but only where the gouts of bronze represented the breaking foam. The dark wave swelled, and turned over into gold, as though breaking on a beach in a bright evening. Held in the overarching topple of the form was the vestigial, barely surfacing form of a man.

'Do you like it?' came Leo's voice behind her.

'Like isn't the word. There isn't a right word.'

'It had to meet the rules for the Barnoon Cemetery, up behind Porthmeor Beach,' he said. 'So I suppose Stella wanted it for herself.'

'No, I don't think so. I think it must have been for Thomas Tremorvah – my father—'

'Well I think you can put up a memorial to someone years after they're dead, if you want to,' he said.

'The funny thing is,' she told him, 'this is in good time.'

'I don't follow you,' he said.

So she told him about it.

'Well then, it must be for him,' he said, when she had done. They were still standing side by side, and looking at the bronze wave.

'I'm sorry it cost so much,' he said. 'It was getting it cast.'

'That doesn't matter,' she said. 'But Leo – weren't you supposed to be off to the Scillies? I didn't expect you to be here.'

'Didn't feel like going alone,' he said. 'Want to come? Carry my gear for me? Better be next week now.'

Marian was silent, the instant negative that had sprung to her lips bitten back.

'I'd be glad if you would,' he said. 'Come, I mean. You don't have to carry things for me. She leaves a hell of a gap.'

'Alice?'

'No. Stella.'

'Let me think – I'll think about it,' she said.

'Oh, did I say there's to be an inscription on that?' he

said, pointing vaguely at his wave. 'Round the plinth. I'll get it cut by a friend who's good at lettering. I take it there isn't any hurry?'

'No. What is it going to say?'

'*Whosoever will save his life shall lose it,*' said Leo.

'Of course,' said Marian. 'I should have known that.'

She began the walk home. On the harbour beach a woman was painting, working at an easel, her box of oils balanced on a folding stool beside her. Marian stopped to watch for a moment. The artist was painting the row of three arches that pierced the quay, and the upturned boats overwintering in a row above them. And of course her gestures were familiar to Marian – the brush upheld, and the thumb marking off a dimension in the view – the dibbling in the paint on the palette, the long considered and then seemingly impulsive sweep of the brush on the canvas—

So that there came to her mind in the same moment the thought that it is those who miss the boat who carry the scars for years, who can never forget, whereas the only man who saved both his life and his honour that night had said simply, 'Why should it be? We aren't here long enough for that,' and in the same moment the recollection of Stella on the wave-crest of the swelling Downs, offering Marian brushes, offering her an easel, smiling.

The empty house was full of light, of perspectives. She walked round it, musing. In Alice's room she straightened the bed, and picked up a book from the floor. A slender volume of poems by Sassoon: *The Heart's Journey*. The flyleaf bore Stella's name, and the date 1930. Below, at some time, Stella had written, 'for Leo'. A postcard marked a page with a poem about a Bach fugue. Marian read it through.

I gaze at my life in a mirror, desirous of good . . .

There was a mirror in her own room. A heavy, full-length mirror on a stand. She pulled it into the bay window, which, like the one in the living room below, gave a triptych prospect of the bay. The mirror filled with light and distances, the open bay, and the far off lighthouse, that lovely monument to altruism, riding its remote rock like a Wallis ship, for the fall of the light gave it the semblance of a jaunty tilt. Marian fetched Stella's paintbox, and the vacant primed canvas, and Alice's music stand to prop it on. She was afraid. She was alone in the cave of flesh, memory's twisting echo-chamber. Across one way out lay human nakedness, across the other rising oblivion. And it was neither her father's absence, nor her mother's abstraction that had hollowed out that cavernous void – it was she herself who had gone missing. She herself who had been lost.

She began to mime Stella – squeezing an array of colours onto the palette, half-filling her tooth-mug with turps. Unnoticed on her shoes and on the floor, the drips of paint began the incursion of chaos. Slowly she turned to face herself. She was standing between the mirror and the light, cast into shadow so that she could discern herself only dimly. But what she wanted to see was truth naked, like the rocks in the tide. It was not something that could be suddenly accomplished. The steepness of the task – it could take the rest of her life – appalled her. She would have to go about it, and about . . . She drew in the dark outline of her own shape. She herself was still obscure to her, but her background was clear – the golden shores, the blue waters of the bright bay, with white water breaking all over it, and a boat – was it the lifeboat?, making out to sea. She dipped her brush into the extruded worm of white, and put on the canvas in front of her a short vertical stroke. For she was desirous of good; she desired it now more than she feared chaos or failure. And if she could bring her picture to any sort of completion, this first mark would represent a vision of the distant lighthouse.